BURIED FOR PLEASURE

BURIED FOR PLEASURE

Edmund Crispin

FELONY & MAYHEM PRESS • NEW YORK

All characters and events portrayed in this work are fictitious.

BURIED FOR PLEASURE

A Felony & Mayhem mystery

PRINTING HISTORY
First UK edition (Victor Gollancz): 1948
First U.S. Edition (Lippincott): 1949
Felony & Mayhem edition: 2009

ISBN 978-1-934609-20-0

Manufactured in the United States of America

Library of Congress Cataloging-in-Publication Data

Crispin, Edmund, 1921-1978.
  Buried for pleasure / Edmund Crispin. -- Felony & Mayhem ed.
     p. cm.
  ISBN-13: 978-1-934609-20-0 (pbk.)
  ISBN-10: 1-934609-20-X (pbk.)
  1. Fen, Gervase (Fictitious character)--Fiction. 2. English teachers--
Fiction. 3. Oxford (England)--Fiction. I. Title.

PR6025.O46B87 2009
823'.912--dc22

                    2008034537

For Peter Oldham

The icon above says you're holding a copy of a book in the Felony & Mayhem "Vintage" category. These books were originally published prior to about 1965, and feature the kind of twisty, ingenious puzzles beloved by fans of Agatha Christie and John Dickson Carr. If you enjoy this book, you may well like other "Vintage" titles from Felony & Mayhem Press.

———◦●◦———

For more about these books, and other Felony & Mayhem titles, or to place an order, please visit our website at

www.FelonyAndMayhem.com

or contact us at

Felony and Mayhem Press
156 Waverly Place
New York, NY 10014

Other "Vintage" Titles from

FELONY&MAYHEM

BURIED FOR PLEASURE

Buried on Monday, buried for health,
Buried on Tuesday, buried for wealth;
Buried on Wednesday, buried at leisure,
Buried on Thursday, buried for pleasure;
Buried on Friday, buried for fun,
Buried on Saturday, buried at one;
Buried on Sunday after eleven,
You get the priest and you go to heaven.

—TRADITIONAL

CHAPTER ONE

"SANFORD ANGELORUM ALL change," said the station-master. "Sanford Angelorum all change."

After a moment's thought: "Terminus," he added, and retired from the scene through a door marked PRIVATE.

Gervase Fen, dozing alone in a narrow, stuffy compartment whose cushions, when stirred, emitted a haze of black dust, woke and roused himself.

He peered out of the window into the summer twilight. A stunted, uneven platform offered itself to his inspection, its further margins cluttered with weed-like growths which a charitable man might have interpreted as attempts at horticulture. An empty chocolate-machine lay rusting and overturned, like a casualty in some robot war. Near it was a packing-case from which the head of a small chicken protruded, uttering low, indignant squawks. But there was no trace of humankind, and beyond the station lay nothing more companionable than an apparently limitless expanse of fields and woods, bluish in the gathering dusk.

This panorama displeased Fen; he thought it blank and unenlivening. There was, however, nothing to be done about it except repine. He repined briefly and then extracted himself and his luggage from the compartment. It seemed at first that he was the only passenger to alight here, but a moment later he found that this was not so, for a fair-haired, neatly dressed girl of about twenty emerged from another compartment, glanced uncertainly about her, and then made for the exit, where she dropped a square of green pasteboard into a tin labelled TICKETS and disappeared. Leaving his luggage where it lay on the platform, Fen followed.

But the station yard—an ill-defined patch of gravel—was empty of conveyances; and except for the retreating footsteps of the girl, who had vanished from sight round a bend in the station approach, a disheartening quietude prevailed. Fen went back to the platform and sought out the station-master's room, where he found the station-master sitting at a table and sombrely contemplating a small unopened bottle of beer. He looked up resignedly at the interruption.

"Is there any chance of my getting a taxi?" Fen asked.

"Where are you for, sir?"

"Sanford Angelorum village. The Fish Inn."

"Well, you might be lucky," the station-master admitted. "I'll see what I can do."

He went to a telephone and discoursed into it. Fen watched from the doorway. Behind him, the train on which he had arrived gave a weak, asthmatic whistle and began to back away. Presently it had disappeared, empty, in the direction whence it came.

The station-master finished his conversation and lumbered back to his chair.

"That'll be all right, sir," he said; and his tone was slightly complacent, as of a midwife relating the successful issue of a troublesome confinement. "Car'll be here in ten minutes."

Fen thanked him, gave him a shilling, and left him still staring at the beer. It occurred to Fen that perhaps he had taken the pledge and was brooding nostalgically over forbidden delights.

The chicken had got its head out of a particularly narrow aperture of the packing-case and was unable to get it in again; it was bewilderedly eyeing a newish election poster, with an unprepossessing photograph, which said: "A Vote for Strode Is a Vote for Prosperity." The train had passed beyond earshot; a colony of rooks was flying home for the night, dark blurs against a grey sky; flickering indistinctly, a bat pursued its evening meal up and down the line. Fen sat down on a suitcase and waited. He had finished one cigarette, and was on the point of lighting another, when the sound of a car engine stirred him into activity. He returned, burdened with cases, to the station yard.

Against all probability, the taxi was new, and comfortable; and its driver, too, was unexpectedly attractive—a slim, comely, black-haired young woman wearing blue slacks and a blue sweater.

"Sorry to keep you waiting," she said pleasantly. "I occasionally meet this train on the offchance that someone will want a car, but there are evenings when no one's on it at all, so it's scarcely worth while...Here, let me give you a hand with your bags."

The luggage was stowed away. Fen asked and obtained permission to sit in front. They set off. In the deepening darkness there was little outside the car to repay attention, and Fen looked instead at his companion, admiring what the dashboard light showed of her large green eyes, her full mouth, her fine and lustrous hair.

"Girls who drive taxis," he ventured, "are surely uncommon?"

She took her eyes momentarily from the road to glance at him; saw a tall, lean man with a ruddy, cheerful, clean-shaven face, and brown hair which stood up mutinously in spikes at the crown of his head. In particular she liked his eyes; they showed charity and understanding as well as a taste for mischief.

"Yes, I suppose they are," she agreed. "But it isn't at all a bad life if you actually own your car, as I do. It's been a good investment."

"You've always done this, then?"

"No. For a time I worked in Boots—the book department. But it didn't suit me, for some reason. I used to get dizzy spells."

"Inevitable, I should think, if you work in a circulating library."

A fallen tree appeared out of the gloom ahead of them; it lay half across the lane. The girl swore mildly, braked, and circumnavigated it with care.

"I always forget that damned thing's there," she said. "It was blown down in a gale, and Shooter ought to have taken it away days ago. It's his tree, so it's his responsibility. But he's really intolerably lax." She accelerated again, asking: "Have you been in this part of the world before?"

"Never," said Fen. "It seems very out-of-the-way," he added reprovingly. His preferences were not bucolic.

"You're staying at the Fish Inn?"

"Yes."

"Well, I ought perhaps to warn you—" The girl checked herself. "No, never mind."

"What's all this?" Fen demanded uneasily. "What were you going to say?"

"It was nothing...How long are you here for?"

"It can't have been *nothing*."

"Well, anyway, there's nowhere else for you to stay, even if you wanted to."

"But *shall* I want to?"

"Yes. No. That's to say, it's an extremely nice pub, only... Oh, damn it, you'll have to see for yourself. How long are you staying?"

Since it was clear that no further enlightenment was to be expected, Fen answered the question. "Till after polling day," he said.

"Oh...You're not Gervase Fen, are you?"

"Yes."

She glanced at him with curiosity. "Yes, I might have known..."

After a pause she went on:

"You're rather late starting your election campaign, you know. There's only a week to go, and I haven't seen a single leaflet about you, or a poster, or anything."

"My agent," said Fen, "is dealing with all that."

The girl considered this reply in silence.

"Look here," she said, "you're a Professor at Oxford, aren't you?"

"Of English."

"Well, what on earth...I mean, *why* are you standing for Parliament? What put the idea into your head?"

Even to himself Fen's actions were sometimes unaccountable, and he could think of no very convincing reply.

"It is my wish," he said sanctimoniously, "to serve the community."

The girl eyed him dubiously.

"Or at least," he amended, "that is one of my motives. Besides, I felt I was getting far too restricted in my interests. Have you ever produced a definitive edition of Langland?"

"Of course not," she said crossly.

"I have. I've just finished producing one. It has queer psychological effects. You begin to wonder if you're mad. And the only remedy for that is a complete change of occupation."

"What it amounts to is that you haven't any serious interest in politics at all," the girl said with unexpected severity.

"Well, no, I wouldn't say that," Fen answered defensively. "My idea, after I've been elected—"

But she shook her head. "You won't be elected, you know."

"Why not?"

"This is a safe Conservative seat. You won't get a look in."

"We shall see."

"You may confuse the issue a little, but you can't affect it ultimately."

"We shall see."

"In fact, you'll be lucky if you don't lose your deposit. What exactly is your platform?"

Fen's confidence waned slightly. "Oh, prosperity," he said, "and exports and freedom and that kind of thing. Will you vote for me?"

"I haven't got a vote—too young. And anyway, I'm canvassing for the Conservatives."

"Oh, dear," said Fen.

They fell silent. Trees and coppices loomed momentarily out of the darkness and were swept away again as though by a giant hand. The headlights gleamed on small flowers sleeping beneath the hedges, and the air of that incomparable summer washed in a warm tide through the open windows. Rabbits, their white scuts bobbing feverishly, fled away to shelter in deep, consoling burrows. And now the lane sloped gently downwards; ahead of them they could glimpse, for the first time, the scattered lights of the village...

With one savage thrust the girl drove the foot-brake down against the boards. The car slewed, flinging them forward, then skidded and at last came safely to a halt. And in the glare of its headlights a human form appeared.

They blinked at it, unable to believe their eyes. It blinked back at them, to all appearance hardly less perturbed than they. Then it waved its arms, uttered a bizarre piping sound, and rushed to the hedge, where it forced its way painfully through a small gap and in another moment, bleeding from a profusion of scratches, was lost from view.

Fen stared after it. "Am I dreaming?" he demanded.

"No, of course not. I saw it too."

"A man—quite a large, young man?"

"In pince-nez?"

"Yes."

"And with no clothes on at all?"

"Yes."

"It seems a little odd," said Fen with restraint.

But the girl had been pondering, and now her initial perplexity gave way to comprehension. "I know what it was," she said. "It was an escaped lunatic."

This explanation struck Fen as conventional, and he said as much.

"No, no," she went on, "the point is that there actually is a lunatic asylum near here, at Sanford Hall."

"On the other hand, it might have been someone who'd been bathing and had had his clothes stolen."

"There's nowhere you can bathe on this side of the village. Besides, I could see that his hair wasn't wet. And didn't he look mad to you?"

"Yes," said Fen without hesitation, "he did. I suppose," he added unenthusiastically, "that I ought really to get out and chase after him."

"He'll be miles away by now. No, we'll tell Sly—that's our constable—when we get to the village, and that's about all we can do."

So they drove on, preoccupied, into Sanford Angelorum, and presently came to the Fish Inn.

CHAPTER TWO

ARCHITECTURALLY, THE FISH Inn did not seem particularly enterprising.

It was a fairly large cube of grey stone, pierced symmetrically by narrow, mean-looking doors and windows, and surrounded by mysterious, indistinguishable heaps of what might be building materials. Its signboard, visible now in the light which filtered from the curtained windows of the bar, depicted murky subaqueous depths set about with sinuous water-weed; against this background a silvery, generalised marine creature, sideways on, was staring impassively at something off the edge of the board.

From within the building, as Fen's taxi drew up at the door, there issued noises suggestive of agitation, and periodically dominated by a vibrant feminine voice.

"It sounds to me as if they've heard about the lunatic," said the girl. "I'll come in with you, in case Sly's there."

The Inn proved to be more prepossessing inside than out. There was only one bar—the tiresome distinction of "lounge" and "public" having been so far-excluded—but it was roomy and spacious, extending half the length and almost all the width of the house. The oak panelling, transferred evidently from some much older building, was carved in the linenfold pattern; faded but still cheerful chintz curtains covered the windows; a heavy beam traversed the ceiling; oak chairs and settles had their discomfort partially mitigated by flat cushions. The decoration consisted largely of indifferent nineteenth-century hunting prints, representing stuffed-looking gentlemen on the backs of fantastically long and emaciated horses; but in addition to these there was, over the fireplace, a canvas so large as to constitute something of a *pièce de résistance*.

It was a seascape, which showed, in the foreground, a narrow strip of shore, up which some men in oilskins were hauling what looked like a primitive lifeboat. To the left was a harbour with a mole, behind which an angry sky suggested the approach of a tornado. And the rest of the available space, which was considerable, was taken up with a stormy sea, flecked with white horses, upon which a number of sailing-ships were proceeding in various directions.

This spirited depiction, Fen was to learn, provided an inexhaustible topic of argument among the habitués of the Inn. From the seaman's point of view, no such scene had ever existed, or could ever exist, on God's earth. But this possibility did not seem to have occurred to anyone at Sanford Angelorum. It was the faith of the inhabitants that if the artist had painted it thus, it must have been thus. And tortuous and implausible modes of navigation had consequently to be postulated in order to explain what was going on. These, it is true, were generally couched in terms which by speakers and auditors alike were only imperfectly understood; but the average Englishman will no more admit ignorance of seafaring matters than he will admit ignorance of women.

"No, no; I tell 'ee, that schooner, 'er's luffin' on the lee shore."

"What about the brig, then? What about the brig?"

"That's no brig, Fred, 'er's a ketch."

"'Er wouldn't be fully-rigged, not if 'er was luffing."

"Look 'ere, take *that* direction as north, see, and that means the wind's nor'-nor'-east."

"Then 'ow the 'ell d'you account for that wave breaking over the mole?"

"That's a current."

"Current, 'e says. Don't be bloody daft, Bert, 'ow can a wave be a current?"

"*Current.* That's a good one."

At the moment when Fen first set eyes on this object, however, it had temporarily lost its hold on the interest of the Inn's clients. This was due to the presence of an elderly lady in a ginger wig who, surrounded by a circle of listeners, was sitting in a collapsed posture on a chair, engaged, between sips of brandy, in vehement and imprecise narration.

"Frightened?" she was saying. "Nearly fell dead in me tracks, I did. There 'e were, all white and nekked, lurking be'ind that clump of gorse by Sweeting's Farm. And jist as I passes by, out 'e jumps at me and 'Boo!' 'e says. 'Boo!'"

At this, an oafish youth giggled feebly.

"And what 'appened then?" someone demanded.

"I struck at 'im," the elderly lady replied, striking illustratively at the air, "with me brolly."

"Did you 'it 'im?"

"No," she admitted with evident reluctance. "'E slip away from me reach, and off 'e went before you could say 'knife.' And 'ow I staggered 'ere I shall never know, not to me dying day. Yes, thank you, Mrs 'Erbert, I'll 'ave another, *if* you please."

"'E must 'a' bin a exhibitor," someone volunteered. "People as goes about showing thesselves in the altogether is called exhibitors."

But this information, savouring as it did of intellectual snobbery, failed to provoke much interest. A middle-aged, bovine, nervous-looking man in the uniform of a police constable, who was standing by with a notebook in his hand, said:

"Well, us all knows what 'tis, I s'pose. 'Tis one o' they loonies escaped from up at 'All."

"These ten years," said a gloomy-looking old man, "I've known that'd 'appen. 'Aven't I said it, time and time again?"

The disgusted silence with which this rhetorical question was received indicated forcibly that he had; with just such repugnance must Cassandra have been regarded at the fall of Troy, for there is something distinctly irritating about a person with an obsession who turns out in the face of all reason to have been right.

The adept in psychological terminology said: "Us ought to organise a search-party, that's what us ought to do. 'E'm likely dangerous."

But the constable shook his head. "Dr Boysenberry'll be seeing to that, I reckon. I'll telephone 'im now, though I've no doubt 'e knows all about it already." He cleared his throat and spoke more loudly. "There is no cause for alarm," he announced. "No cause for alarm at all."

The Inn's clients, who had shown not the smallest evidence of such an emotion, received this statement apathetically, with the single exception of the elderly lady in the wig, who by now was slightly contumelious from brandy.

"Tcha!" she exclaimed. "That's just like 'ee, Will Sly. An ostrich, that's what you are, with your 'ead buried in sand. No cause for alarm, *in*deed! If it'd bin you 'e'd jumped out at, you'd not go about saying there was 'no cause for alarm.' There 'e were, white and nekked like an evil sperrit..."

Her audience, however, was clearly not anxious for a repetition of the history; it began to disperse, resuming abandoned glasses and tankards. The gloomy-looking old man buttonholed people with complacent iterations of his own foresight. The psychologist embarked on a detailed and scabrous account, in low tones and to an exclusively male circle, of the habits of exhibitors. And Constable Sly, on the point of commandeering the Inn's telephone, caught the eye of the girl from the taxi for the first time since she and Fen had entered the bar.

" 'Ullo, Miss Diana," he said, grinning awkwardly. "You've 'eard what's 'appened, I s'pose?"

"I have, Will," said Diana, "and I think I may be able to help you a bit." She related their encounter with the lunatic.

"Ah," said Sly. "That may be very useful, Miss Diana. 'E were making for Sanford Condover, you say?"

"As far as I could tell, yes."

"I will inform Dr Boysenberry of that fact," said Sly laboriously. He turned to the woman who was serving behind the bar. "All right for I to use 'phone, Myra?"

"You can use the phone, my dear," Myra Herbert said, "if you put tuppence in the box." She was a vivacious and attractive Cockney woman in the middle thirties, with black hair, a shrewd but slightly sensual mouth, and green eyes unusually but beautifully shaped.

"Official call," Sly explained with hauteur.

Myra registered disgust. "You and your official ruddy calls," she said. "My God."

Sly ignored this and turned away; at which the lunatic's first victim, becoming suddenly aware of his impeding departure, roused herself from an access of lethargy to say: "And what about me, Will Sly?"

Sly grew harassed. "Well, Mrs 'Ennessy, what *about* you?"

"You're not going to leave me to walk 'ome by meself, I should 'ope."

"I've already explained to you, Mrs 'Ennessy," said Sly with painful dignity, "that there is no cause for alarm."

Mrs Hennessy emitted a shriek of stage laughter.

"Listen to 'im," she adjured Fen, who was contemplating his potential constituents with a hypnotised air: "Listen to Mr Knowall Sly!" Her manner changed abruptly to one of menace. "For all you knows, Will Sly, I might be murdered on me own doorstep, like that poor French lady as was poisoned through the post, and *then* where'd you be? I got a right to pertection, 'aven't I ? I got—"

"Now, look 'ere, Mrs 'Ennessy, I've me duty to do."

"Duty!" Mrs Hennessy repeated with scorn. " 'E says—" and here she again addressed Fen, this time with the air of one imparting a valuable confidence—" 'e says 'e's got 'is duty to do…Fat lot of duty you do, Will Sly. What about the time Alf Braddock's apples was stolen? Eh? What about that? *Duty!*"

"Yes, duty," said Sly, much aggrieved at this unsportsman-like allusion. "And what's more, the next time I catch you trying to buy Guinness 'ere out of hours—"

Diana interrupted these indiscretions.

"It's all right, Will," she said. "I'll take Mrs Hennessy home. It's not far out of my way."

The offer restored peace and a semblance of amity. Sly went to the telephone. Fen paid Diana and retrieved his luggage from the taxi. Myra called time. The company grudgingly finished its drinks and departed, Diana enduring with angelic patience a new and more highly coloured account of Mrs Hennessy's adventure.

Fen introduced himself to Myra, signed a register and was shown to his room, which was comfortable and scrupulously clean. He ordered, obtained and consumed beer, coffee and sandwiches.

"And I should like," he told Myra, "to be allowed to sleep on till ten tomorrow morning."

At this, to his mystification, Myra laughed very happily; and, controlling herself at length, said: "Very well, my dear: good night," and tripped gracefully from the room, leaving him theorising gloomily about what her unexpected reaction might mean.

There remained, for that evening, only one further incident which interested him. His visit to the bathroom gave him a glimpse of someone who was vaguely familiar—a thin, auburn-haired man of about his own age whom he saw vanishing in a dressing-gown into one of the other bedrooms. But the association which was so certainly in his mind refused to reveal itself, and though he pondered the problem while getting into bed, he soon abandoned it for lack of inspiration, and by the time the Church clock struck midnight was sound asleep.

CHAPTER THREE

HE WAS HORRIBLY awakened, in what seemed about ten minutes, by an outbreak of intensive hammering somewhere in the regions below.

He groped for his watch, focussed his eyes with difficulty on its dial, and perceived that the time was only seven. Outside the bedroom windows the sun was shining brilliantly. Fen eyed it with displeasure. He was temperamentally a late riser, and the *panache* of virgin daylight made little appeal to him.

Meanwhile, the noise below was increasing in volume and variety, as if fresh recruits were arriving momently. And now it became clear to Fen's fuddled mind that in this lay, probably, the reason both for Diana's gnomic warning and for Myra's irrepressible hilarity of the previous evening, when he had said he wished to sleep late. He uttered a groan of dismay.

It acted like a signal.

There came a tap on his door, and in response to his croak of invitation a girl entered so superlatively beautiful that Fen began to wonder if he were dreaming.

The girl was a natural platinum blonde. Her features were flawless. She had a figure like the quintessence of all pin-up girls. And she moved with an unselfconscious and quite unprovocative placidity which made it evident that—incredible though it might seem—she was quite unaware of her perfections.

With a radiant smile she deposited a tray of tea on the bedside table; left the room; returned presently with his shoes, beautifully polished; smiled at him again; and the next moment, like a fairy-tale vision—though he could imagine no princess of the Perilous Realm capable of offering her lover such nuptial joys as this—was gone.

Dazed, Fen lit his early-morning cigarette; and the familiar unpleasantness of smoking it restored him to something like normalcy. He sipped tea—and as he did so there drifted into the hazy miasma of his thoughts the recollection of certain words that had been spoken last night; a French lady, poisoned through the post…It was possible of course, that this had been mere rhetoric. Still, it might perhaps be worth further enquiry? Or, after all, would it be beneath one's dignity to…

But at this point the hammering, continuing unabated, was interrupted by a noise which sounded like a very large scaffolding giving way. Fen got up hurriedly, washed, shaved, dressed and went downstairs.

The whole household was astir—as, unless heavily drugged, it could hardly fail to be. Fen found Myra out in the yard, contemplating a small, greyish, unalluring pig which seemed to be trying to make up its mind how to employ the day.

"Good morning, my dear," Myra greeted him brightly. "Sleep well?"

"Up to a point," said Fen with reserve.

She indicated the pig. "Did you ever see anything like him?" she asked.

"Well, no, now you mention it, I don't think I have."

"I've been cheated," said Myra, and the pig grunted, apparently in assent. "I like a young pig to be nice and pink, you know, and cheerful-like. But him—my God. I feed him and feed him, but he never grows."

They meditated jointly on this phenomenon. A passing farm-labourer joined them.

" 'E don't get no bigger, do 'e?" he observed.

"What's the matter with him, Alf?"

The farm-labourer pondered. " 'E'm a non-doer," he diagnosed at last.

"A what?"

"Non-doer. You're wasting your time trying to fatten 'im. 'E'll never got no larger. Better sell 'im."

"Non-doer," said Myra with disgust. "That's a nice cheerful ruddy thought to start the day with."

The farm-labourer departed.

"I'll say this for him, though," said Myra, referring to the pig, "he's very affectionate, which is a point in his favour, I suppose."

They turned back to the Inn. Myra suggested that Fen might now like to have breakfast, and Fen agreed.

"But what is happening?" he demanded, indicating the hammering.

"Renovations, my dear. They're renovating the interior."

"But workmen never get started as early as this."

"Oh, it isn't workmen," said Myra obscurely. "That's to say..."

They came to a door in a part of the ground floor with which Fen was not yet acquainted, and from behind which most of the din seemed to be proceeding. "Look," said Myra.

The opening of the door disclosed a dense cloud of plaster dust in which figures could dimly be discerned engaged, to all appearance, in a labour of unqualified destruction. One of these—a man—loomed up at them suddenly, looking like a whitewash victim in a slapstick comedy.

"Morning, Myra," he said with disarming heartiness. "Everything all right?"

"Oh, quite, sir." Myra was distinctly bland and respectful. "This gentleman's staying here, and he wondered what was going on."

"Morning to you, sir," said the man. "Hope we didn't get you up too early."

"Not a bit," Fen replied without cordiality.

"I feel better already—" the man spoke, however, more with determination than with conviction—"for getting up at six every morning...It's one of the highroads to health, as I've always said."

He fell into a violent fit of coughing; his face became red, and then blue. Fen banged him prophylactically between the shoulder-blades.

"Well, back to the grindstone," he said when he had recovered a little. "I'll tell you this much, sir, there's a good deal to be said, when you want a thing done, for doing it yourself." Someone caught him a glancing blow on the arm with a small pick. "Careful, damn you, that hurt..."

He left them in order to expostulate in more detail. They closed the door and continued on their way.

"Who was that?" Fen asked.

"Mr Beaver, who owns the pub. I only manage it for him. He's a wholesale draper, really."

"I see," said Fen, who saw nothing.

"Have your breakfast now, my dear," Myra soothed him, "and I'll explain later."

She conducted him to a small room where there was a table laid for three. Here, to his elation, she provided him with bacon, eggs and coffee.

He had finished these, and come to the marmalade stage, when the door opened and he was surprised to see the fair-haired girl who had been his sole fellow-passenger on the train.

He studied her covertly as she sat down at the table. Though she had neither Diana's fresh, open-air charm nor Myra's vivacity nor his blonde visitant's filmic radiance, she was none the less pretty in a shy, quiet fashion; and her features showed what seemed to be a mingling of two, distinct strains. The nose, for instance, was markedly patrician, while by contrast the large mouth hinted at vulgarity; the set of the eyebrows was arrogant but the eyes were timid; and it occurred to Fen, in a burst of rather dreary fancifulness which only the unnaturally early hour can excuse, that if a king were to marry a courtesan, a daughter very much like this might be born to them.

It seemed to him, too, that the girl was nervous, rather as if she were about to face some new and testing experience of which the issue was uncertain. And her clothes confirmed this notion. They were good and tasteful, but something in the way she wore them suggested that they were her cared-for best, that she could not always afford to dress thus, that she was wearing them now—yes, that was it—in the hope of making a good impression.

On whom? Fen wondered. A potential employer, perhaps. Her being here to be interviewed for a coveted job would explain her nervousness plausibly enough...

Or, after all, would it? Somehow he sensed that the testing was to be at once more urgent and more intimate than that.

They talked a little, on conventional topics. Fen asked her if she had heard about the lunatic, and on discovering that she had not, explained the situation to her. However, her responses, though polite and intelligent enough, showed that she was too preoccupied to be very much interested in the subject.

He noted that she watched him steadily whenever he spoke, as if trying to assess his character from his expression. And in the fashion of her own speech there was further matter for surmise, since she pronounced her words in a slightly foreign fashion which he found himself unable to identify. She was not—to judge from that—German or Italian or French or Dutch or Spanish; nor was there any immingled trace of dialect which might account for the oddity of the effect. Analysed, it came to this, that while her vowel-sounds were pure and accurate, there was a very slight tendency to blur and confuse the individual constituents of each group of consonants—labials, gutturals, sibilants. Thus, "p" was not entirely distinct from "b," nor "s" from "z."

Fen discovered that he was incapable of explaining this, and the effect was to make him slightly peevish.

He finished his coffee and looked at his watch. Half past eight. In three hours he had an appointment with his election agent, but until then he was free to do what he pleased. And since the tumult of renovation made the Fish Inn uninhabitable for long at a time, he decided to go out into the sunshine to inspect his constituency at first hand. He therefore took his leave of the girl, suspecting—though without rancour—that she was not sorry to be rid of him.

Outside the door he encountered Myra, and asked for news of the lunatic.

"Well, they haven't caught him, my dear," she said, "though the asylum people have been traipsing about the neighbourhood all night."

"It actually *was* a lunatic, then?"

"Oh, yes. I didn't think it was at first. Mrs Hennessy's just the sort of daft old woman to have—what d'you call them?—sexual delusions about naked men jumping out at her in the dark."

"But I saw him too," Fen pointed out.

Myra's expression suggested that only politeness had prevented her from attributing sexual delusions to Fen also.

"Anyway, he's real enough," she said, "and they've put out he's harmless, though of course they couldn't very well say he was homicidal for fear of creating a panic. And what I say about lunatics is this: They wouldn't be lunatics if you knew what they were going to be up to next."

With this sombre prognosis she left Fen, informing him parenthetically that the bar would be open at eleven.

He was about to go out when his attention was caught by the Inn register, which lay on a table almost at his elbow. Opening it, he found that the girl with whom he had break-fasted was named Jane Persimmons, that she was British, and that she lived at an address in Nottingham. And it struck him that here also he might get enlightenment about the man he had glimpsed the previous evening and whose appearance had seemed vaguely familiar.

He turned back the page and read with some interest the entry immediately preceding his own. It ran:

Major Rawdon Crawley, British, 201, Curzon Street, London.

"Good God," Fen murmured to himself. "Either he just doesn't care, or else he imagines that no one in this district has ever read Thackeray...Well, well, it's none of my business, I suppose."

He noted that the *soi-disant* Crawley had arrived two days previously, closed the book, and went out into the Inn yard.

There was no cloud in the sky, but a brief shower during the night had mitigated the dust accumulated during weeks of drought and painted grass, leaves and hedges a fresher and more lively green. The non-doing pig was noisily eating pota-toes. Fen crossed the yard and came out into the main street of the village.

Before setting out for the district he had studied Ordnance Survey maps, and so he was able to orientate himself fairly easily. The district is an agglomeration of Sanfords, presided over by Sanford Hall, which stands isolated on one of the few eminences which that very level county can claim. Rich pasture extends uninterruptedly almost as far as the Marlock Hills, though here and there you may see little rashes of barley, to which the soil is unsuited but which protesting farmers have been obliged to put in by ill-informed *fiats* from the Ministry of Agriculture. The river Spoor, here only twenty miles from its source, meanders amiably between willows and alders, its waters reputedly inimical to fish. It is fed by a small, erratic tributary, very liable to drought, which runs down from a lake in the grounds of Sanford Hall.

Sanford Morvel is the chief town. It has no function except as a market for neighbouring farmers, and this parasitic existence gives it a blustering, unconfident air. Four miles to the south-east of it is Sanford Condover, less a defined community than a fortuitous collection of small farms loosely plastered together by some cottages, a Baptist chapel and an unsightly pub. Six miles to the south of that is Sanford Angelorum.

A small branch line of the Great Western Railway proceeds reluctantly as far as Sanford Morvel, and an even smaller branch line proceeds even more reluctantly from Sanford Morvel to within two miles of Sanford Angelorum (taking in an almost totally disused halt at Sanford Condover on the way), where it suddenly peters out, the Company, with the optimism engendered by nineteenth-century industrial progress, having built the line thus far on the assumption that the then Lord Sanford would allow them to continue right up to the village. This supposition, however, proved to be mistaken, since the then Lord Sanford was a disciple of William Morris and nourished a fanatical hatred of railways. The station at which Fen had arrived consequently stands, futile and alone, at a place from which no human dwelling is even visible, and though amended laws would now permit the railway to carry out its original project, it has long since lost interest in the matter.

In the normal way Fen would have made Sanford Morvel his headquarters, since it is admittedly the central point of the constituency. But he had entered the political arena cavalierly and late, to find the housing shortage in Sanford Morvel so acute that neither a committee room nor a bedroom could be found for him. He had therefore been obliged to choose between Sanford Angelorum and a slum-like place, twelve miles to the north of Sanford Morvel, named Peek. Peek, an affair of mean grey semi-detached houses, sprang up in the eighteen-fifties as a result of the discovery of a seam of inferior coal. It declined, some twenty years later, as a result of the working out of that seam, which to the irritation of those who had financed it proved to be minute. The mining community, for which Peek had been built, departed; the more thriftless elements of the district took over; and Peek, its *raison d'être* gone, decayed with startling rapidity.

Of all this Fen had deviously apprised himself. Peek, for his purposes, was clearly impossible. And, surveying Sanford Angelorum in the clear summer light, he was glad he had elected to stay in that charming, unpretentious village.

He admired it as he walked along the main street in the direction opposite to that of the railway station. Like most such places, it was assembled, he saw, round the Church, a medium-good example of the Decorated style whose ornamental conceits, being carved in red sandstone, were a good deal blurred by weathering. The Rectory, built large for an age more opulent and more philoprogenitive than this, adjoined it. There were one or two shops; there was a green with a War Memorial; there was a row of delightful eighteenth-century cottages; there was, obstinately Victorian, the Fish Inn.

Outside the gate of one of the cottages Fen saw Diana talking earnestly to a young man in shabby tweeds. She waved to him, but her conversation seemed engrossing, and he did not venture to interrupt it.

Before long he reached the edge of the village and came to a spot which he suspected might be the scene of Mrs Hennessy's encounter on the previous evening. Resisting the temptation to root about for traces of the lunatic, he passed on, and soon arrived at a miniature cross-roads, with a signpost which added to its total illegibility the even graver defect of pointing in no particular direction.

After some hesitation he entered the lane on the left.

It was the height of summer. The hips of the dogrose were ripe in the hedges. Barley was being cut, flecked with the scarlet of poppies. Copper butterflies foamed fragile as thistle-down through the hot air. Spiders' webs draped the twigs and leaves. In the distance a heat haze was forming, but a line of white smoke enabled you to follow the progress of a distant train.

Fen began to walk more briskly. The country, a place with which he was not normally infatuated, seemed particularly winning today…

But he had not gone a hundred yards before a startling spectacle halted him in his tracks.

CHAPTER FOUR

HE HAD COME to a five-barred gate giving access to a large, irregularly shaped field. Its hedges were mainly of thorn. It had a dank-looking pond—much diminished now by the lack of rain—in the middle of it. And at the pond's margin a duck, its snow-white plumage somewhat marred by the green slime which clung to its underside, was hobbling slowly about.

But it was not these things that had caught Fen's attention. It was a man who was entering the field through a gap on the far side.

He was short, stout, harassed-looking, middle-aged. He wore gloves, a reefer jacket inside out, and pale purple trousers tucked into large black gumboots. And he was moving in a crouched, furtive manner, like one who tries to evade pursuit.

On reaching the edge of the pond, however, he straightened up and glanced quickly about him; then produced from the pocket of his coat a large, antique service revolver which seemed to be attached by a length of string to his braces. This he levelled at a wizened sapling which was growing by the hedge.

"Bang," he said. "Bang, bang, bang."

Now a look of satisfaction appeared on his face, and, turning, he suddenly hurled the revolver, still attached to its string, into the centre of the pond. After a moment's pause he hauled it out again, like a fish on the end of a line, removed the string both from it and from his braces, wrapped this string in a piece of newspaper, crammed it into his pocket and, leaving the revolver where it lay, hurried across to the sapling, where with much difficulty he shouldered an imaginary burden and tottered with it in Fen's direction. The duck, which had ambled into his path, gave him one look and then fled away before him, quacking angrily, like a leaf driven by an autumn gale.

It was clear that the man had not yet become aware of Fen's presence. He staggered almost as far as the gate, lowered his invisible load to the ground with a sigh of relief, pulled off his coat, removed the paper-wrapped length of string from its pocket, turned the coat delicately right side out, and with much groaning and effort began putting it on to whatever it was he imagined was lying at his feet.

He was thus engaged when, becoming abruptly conscious that he was not alone, he looked up and caught Fen's fascinated eye.

He stood upright, slowly, and expelled his breath in a long gasp of dismay.

"A-aaaaaah," he said.

They gazed rigidly at one another for a moment longer. Then the man, recovering the power of articulate speech, remarked: "I'm not mad."

This discouraging social gambit touched Fen. He said kindly: "Of course you're not mad."

The man became frantic. "I'm *really* not mad, I mean," he said.

"I quite believe you," said Fen. "You needn't imagine I'm just trying to humour you."

"You see," the man nervously explained, "there's a lunatic at large, and I was afraid that you, being a stranger, might assume—"

"No, no," Fen reassured him. "I never had any doubt about what you were doing. But I imagine few detective novelists can be as scrupulous."

The man relaxed suddenly, and began wiping his forehead with a brightly coloured handkerchief. He picked up the reefer jacket and put it on.

"One's plots are necessarily *improbable*," he said a trifle didactically, "but I believe in making sure that they are not *impossible*." His utterance was prim and self-conscious, like himself. "Short of the murder itself, I try everything out before finally adopting it for a book, and really, you would be surprised at the number of flaws and difficulties which are revealed in the process."

Fen put his elbows on the top bar of the gate and leaned there comfortably.

"And of course," he said, "it must enable you to get to some extent inside the mind of the murderer."

An expression of mild repugnance appeared on the man's face. "No," he said, "no, it doesn't do that." The subject seemed painful to him, and Fen felt that he had committed an indiscretion. "The fact is," the man went on, "that I have no interest in the minds of murderers, or for that matter," he added rather wildly, "in the minds of anyone else. Characterisation seems to me a very over-rated element in fiction. I can never see why one should be obliged to have any of it at all, if one doesn't want to. It *limits* the form so."

Fen agreed, with no special conviction, that it did, and particularly in the case of detective stories. "I read a good many of them," he said, "and I must know yours. May I ask your name?"

"Judd," the man replied, "my name is Judd. But I write—" he hesitated, in some embarrassment—"I write under the pseudonym of 'Annette de la Tour.'"

"Ah, yes," said Fen. Annette de la Tour's books, he remembered, were complicated, lurid and splendidly melodramatic. And certainly they made no concessions to the Baal of characterisation. He said: "Your work has given me a great deal of pleasure, Mr Judd."

"Has it?" said Mr Judd eagerly. "Has it really? I've been writing for twenty years, and no one has ever said anything like that to me before. My dear fellow, I'm so grateful." His eyes sparkled with innocent pleasure. "And it's all the better coming, as it evidently does, from an intelligent man."

Upon this shameless *quid pro quo* he paused expectantly; and Fen, feeling that he was required to identify himself, did so. Mr Judd slapped his hands together with excitement.

"But how splendid!" he exclaimed. "Of course I've followed all your cases. We must have a very long talk together, a very long talk indeed. Are you staying here?"

"Yes."

"For long?"

"Until after polling day. I'm standing for Parliament."

Mr Judd was taken aback.

"*Standing*?" he repeated dazedly. "For *Parliament*?"

"It is my wish to serve the community," Fen said. Confronted with this pronouncement, Mr Judd showed himself either more credulous or more courteous than Diana had been.

"Very commendable," he murmured. "To tell you the truth, I had rather forgotten there was a by-election in progress...What interest do you represent?"

"I'm an Independent."

"Then you shall have my vote," said Mr Judd, narrowly forestalling a primitive attempt at canvassing on Fen's part.

"And if I had fifty votes," he added lyrically, "you should have them all. Tell me, which of my books do you think the best?"

Fen rummaged in his mind, seeking not for that book of Mr Judd's which he thought the best, but for the one which Mr Judd was likely to cherish most. "*The Screaming Bone*," he said at last.

"Admirable!" said Mr Judd, and Fen was pleased that his diagnosis had been correct. "I'm so glad you enjoyed that one, because the critics were very down on it and yet I've always thought it the finest thing I've done. Mind you, the critics are down on all my books, because they haven't any psychology in them, but they were particularly harsh about that one...You're very perceptive, Professor Fen, very perceptive indeed." He beamed approval. "Still, we mustn't waste time talking about my nonsense," he concluded insincerely. "Where are you heading for?"

"I think"—Fen glanced at his watch—"that it's about time I was strolling back to the village."

Mr Judd's face fell. "What a pity—I have to go in the opposite direction, or we could have walked along together and talked," he said with great simplicity, "about my books. Still, you must come and have a meal with me—I live in a cottage only a quarter of a mile from here. What about lunch today?"

Fen said: "I'm afraid, you know, that I'm going to be very busy during the coming week," but Mr Judd's disappointment was so manifest and poignant that he was moved to add: "But I dare say we can fit something in."

"Please try," said Mr Judd earnestly. "Please try. My telephone number is Sanford 13, and you needn't hesitate to ring me at any time. Where are you staying?"

"The Fish Inn," said Fen.

These words produced, unexpectedly enough, a marked change in Mr Judd. A new light appeared in his eyes—a light which Fen could not but associate with the more disreputable antics of satyrs in classic woods. In tones of reverence he said:

"The Fish Inn...Tell me, have you come across that beautiful girl?"

"The blonde?"

"The blonde."

"Well, yes. She brought me my early-morning tea."

Mr Judd drew in his breath sharply.

"She brought you your *tea*," he said, somehow investing Fen's prosaic statement with the glamour of a phallic rite. "And was she wearing that powder-blue frock?"

"I can't really remember," said Fen vaguely. "It was something tight-fitting, I think."

"*Tight-fitting*," Mr Judd repeated with awe. He looked at Fen as he might have looked at a man who had lit a fire with bank-notes. "Do you know, I think she's the most beautiful girl I've ever seen...Do you think she reads my books? I've never dared ask her."

"I doubt if she's intelligent enough to read anyone's books."

Mr Judd sighed. "It's just as well, perhaps," he said, "because she mightn't like them..." He veered from the topic with obvious reluctance. "Well, well, I mustn't keep you."

"Don't forget your revolver," said Fen.

"No, I'd better not do that. Apart from anything else, I haven't got a licence for it."

"And by the way—what is the point of throwing it into the pond and pulling it out again?"

"That," Mr Judd explained, "is because the murderer wants to give the impression that he left it there at the time of the murder, and only retrieved it *a good deal later*, for fear of its discovery. The detective, of course, finds it somewhere quite different."

"But why should the murderer want to give that impression?"

Mr Judd became evasive. "I think you'd better read the book when it comes out. I'll send you a copy...You realise about the coat, of course. It belongs to the victim, and the murderer wears it inside out so that when he carries the body the coat gets bloodstains on it where they ought to be, on the inside."

"Yes," said Fen. "Yes, I'd grasped that."

"Very quick of you. Well, you'll let me know when you can pay me a visit, won't you? I shall look forward to it, look forward to it enormously. I live a very solitary life, because there's no one intelligent to talk to in Sanford Angelorum except the Rector, and his interests are confined to theology and birds and gardening, about all of which his information is tiresomely complete. Yes, you must certainly come and have a meal, and I shall be interested to hear any criticisms you may have to make about my books...Yes, well, goodbye for the present."

"Goodbye," said Fen, shaking him by the hand. "I've very much enjoyed meeting you, and I hope I didn't interrupt your test."

"Not in the least," Mr Judd assured him. "All I had left to do was to take the body into the village and put it on top of the War Memorial...Well, then, I shall hope to be seeing you."

CHAPTER FIVE

THEY PARTED CORDIALLY, Mr Judd to retrieve his revolver and Fen to return to the village, full of regret at having missed seeing Mr Judd hoisting an imaginary corpse onto the War Memorial, and speculating on Mr Judd's murderer's motives in performing this laborious and public act.

He had reached the point provisionally identified as Sweeting's Farm, and had worked out a rambling, intricate theory about Mr Judd's murderer which involved the propinquity of an expatriate tulip-grower from Harlingen, when he saw approaching him, at a slow and thoughtful pace, the self-styled Crawley, who was now wearing a tweed cap and a tweed knickerbocker suit and carrying a fishing-rod in a manner which suggested that he was unused to it.

The conviction of having seen or known this man in some other context returned to Fen with redoubled force. He decided to accost him and if possible resolve the problem.

In this project, however, he was over-sanguine. The man looked up, observed his purposeful approach, glanced hurriedly about him, and in another moment had bounded over a stile and was hastening precipitately away across the field to which it gave access.

Shaken at being thus obviously avoided, Fen halted; then resumed his walk in a less cheerful mood. At one time and another he had made contact with various persons whom the law regarded with disfavour, and it was not impossible that "Crawley" was one of them. In that case Fen had a responsibility for preventing whatever mischief might be contemplated—only the trouble was that he could not be sure that any mischief *was* contemplated...

He inspected the miscellaneous lumber-room of his mind in the hope of enlightenment, but vainly. He was still inspecting it, still vainly, when he arrived back at the Inn.

His walk had taken him longer than he imagined, and it was already ten past eleven. The bar, however, got little custom before mid-day, and it was empty except for Myra, for the blonde, and for a sullen-looking, Cold-Comfort-Farmish sort of man who was looming across at Myra and speaking slowly but with great vehemence.

"I'll 'ave 'ee," he was saying. "I'll get 'ee, see if I doan't."

He pointed a dramatic finger at Myra, who nevertheless did not seem much perturbed. "Don't be so ruddy daft, Sam," she said.

"I doan mind you'm being a barmaid," the Cold-Comfort-Farmish man resumed graciously. "I'm not one o' your proud uns. Come on, Myra, be a sport. 'T woan't take not five minutes."

Myra, unmoved by this promise of despatch, indicated Fen.

"You're making a fool of yourself in front of the gentleman, Sam," she said. "Finish your drink like a good boy and go back to the farm. I know you didn't ought to be here, and you'll cop it if Farmer Bligh finds out."

The passionate rustic turned upon Fen a look of intense hatred, emptied his glass, wiped his mouth, muttered something derogatory to womanhood and strode out of the bar. In a moment he reappeared outside the window, which was slightly grimy, traced on it with his forefinger the words I LOVE YOU in reverse, so that they could be read from inside, glowered at them all and went away.

"That's clever," said Myra, in reference apparently to the calligraphic feat. "He must have been practising it at home."

"Ah," said Fen noncommittally.

"Of course, Sam, he's a chronic case—been carrying on like that for nearly two years now. It's flattering in a way, but I can't think how he doesn't get sick of it."

"I suppose," said Fen, with hazy recollections of novels about bucolic communities, "that time doesn't mean very much to him."

"What would you like to drink, my dear?"

"A pint of bitter, please. And you?"

"Oh, thank you, sir, I'll have a Worthington, if I may." Fen settled on a stool by the bar, and while they drank talked to Myra about the people he had met in Sanford Angelorum.

Of Diana he learned that she was an orphan—the daughter of a former local G. P. who had died almost penniless through never sending in bills—that she was much liked by the local people, and that she was reputed to be in love with young Lord Sanford.

Of young Lord Sanford he learned that he was in his last year at Oxford, that he was a zealous Socialist, that he lived not in Sanford Hall itself but in the dower-house attached to it, that the local people would have liked him better if he had not been so conscientiously democratic, and that he might or might not be going to marry Diana.

Of Sanford Hall he learned that young Lord Sanford had presented it to the Nation, and that the Nation had promptly turned it into a mental asylum run by the Home Office.

Of Mr Judd he learned that he kept himself to himself.

Of Myra he learned that her husband had died five years previously and that she liked working in pubs.

Of Mr Beaver he learned that he was a man of great initial determination but little staying-power.

Of Jane Persimmons he learned that she was very quiet and reserved, that she had not disclosed her business in the village, that Myra liked her, and that she was fairly certainly not well off.

"Then she's a stranger in the district?" Fen asked.

"Yes, my dear. And the man is, too—Crawley, I mean. Have you seen him yet?"

Fen said that he had.

"He's a queer one," Myra went on. "Came here three days ago. Off on his own all day and every day—sometimes doesn't even have breakfast. Says he goes fishing, but no one ever comes here to fish: there's nothing in the Spoor but two or three minnows. And anyway, it's obvious he knows no more about fishing than my backside. He's a mystery, he is. Jacqueline mistrusted him from the start—didn't you, Jackie?" she said to the blonde barmaid.

Jacqueline, who was patiently polishing glasses, nodded and favoured them with a radiant smile. Fen noted, for Mr Judd's future information, that she was wearing a plain black frock with white at the wrists and neck, and a rather beautiful old marcasite brooch.

Myra was regarding her with considerable fondness.

"Isn't she lovely?" said Myra with proprietary pride. "Talk about dumb ruddy blondes."

The dumb ruddy blonde, unembarrassed, glowed at them again, like a large electric bulb raised gently to its fullest power and then as gently dimmed.

"And she's everything you imagine blondes with figures aren't," said Myra. "Goes to church regular, looks after her pa and ma in Sanford Morvel, doesn't smoke or drink, and hardly ever goes out with men. But of course, the only thing people want to do is just look at her—almost the only thing, that is," Myra corrected herself in the interests of accuracy.

Jacqueline smiled exquisitely a third time, and continued peaceably to polish glasses. A customer came in, and Myra abandoned Fen in order to attend to him. At the time of Fen's return to the Inn, all had been quiet. But now a light tapping from some other quarter of the building indicated that Mr Beaver's interregnum, whatever might have been its cause, was over. The tapping grew rapidly in vehemence, and was soon joined, fugally, by other similar noises.

"My God," said Myra. "They're off again."

Fen thought the moment appropriate to demand an explanation of the repairs.

"It's quite simple, my dear," said Myra. "In the normal way we only get the locals in here, and of course that means the pub doesn't make much money. So Mr Beaver decided he'd like to turn it into a sort of roadhouse place, swanky-like, you know, and expensive, and get people to come here in their cars from all over the county."

"But that's a deplorable ambition," Fen protested.

"Well, you can understand it, can't you?" said Myra tolerantly. "I know there's some as say the village ought to stay unspoiled, and all that, but it's my opinion that if people aren't allowed to make as much money as they can, we shall all be worse off."

Fen considered this fiscal theory and decided that, subject to a good deal of qualification, there was something in it.

"But still," he said, "it does seem a pity. You know the sort of customers you'll get: loud-voiced, red-faced men with Hudson Terraplanes and toothbrush moustaches, and little slinky girls with geranium lips and an eye to the main chance smoking cigarettes in holders."

Myra sighed a little at this vision of the coming Gomorrah, but—since unlike Fen she was not prone to aesthetic bigotry—did not seem, he thought, to be seriously dismayed.

"Anyway," she said, "it's their pub to do what they like with. They tried to get a licence for the renovations, but the Ministry refused it. So they're doing the whole thing themselves."

"Doing it themselves?"

"There's a regulation, you see, that if you don't employ workmen and don't spend more than a hundred pounds, you can do up your house, or whatever it is, yourself. Mr Beaver's got his whole family at it, and some of his friends drop in now and again to lend a hand."

"Surely, though, it's a job for an expert."

"Ah," said Myra rather sombrely. "You're right there, my dear. But that's Mr Beaver all over. Once he gets an idea into his head, nothing'll stop him. And if you ask me—"

But what more she would have said Fen never learned. Even as she spoke, he had been conscious that a large and noisy car was pulling up at the door of the Inn.

And now, with the consciously grandiose air of a god from a machine, a newcomer strode into the bar.

CHAPTER SIX

THE NEWCOMER WAS a man of between thirty and forty, though a certain severity of expression made him seem rather older. He was tall and stringy, with a weather-beaten complexion, a long straight nose, bright, bird-like eyes, and thin brown hair which glistened with bay rum; and he wore jodhpurs, riding-boots, a violent check hacking coat, and a yellow tie with horses' heads on it. In his hand he carried a green pork-pie hat with ventilation-holes in the top, so that it looked as if someone had been shooting at him.

He stalked to the bar, rapped on it, and demanded peremptorily to be told if Professor Fen were available.

"I am Fen," said Fen.

The newcomer's manner changed at once to one of great affability. He took Fen's hand and joggled it up and down prolongedly.

"My dear sir," he said, "this is a very great pleasure. Damme, yes. Delighted, and all that…What are you having?"

"Bitter, I think."

"A pint of bitter, miss, and a large Scotch for me."

"You are Captain Watkyn?" Fen asked mistrustfully.

"You've got it in one, old boy," said Captain Watkyn with enthusiasm; it was as though he were commending Fen for the solution of a particularly awkward riddle. "The old firm in person, at your service now as always...Well, bung-ho."

They drank.

"It's a good thing you're a drinking man," Captain Watkyn added pensively. "I had to act for a T. T. once—Melton Mowbray, I think it was—and between ourselves, I had a pretty sticky time of it."

"Did he get in?"

"No," said Captain Watkyn with satisfaction, "he didn't. Mind you," he went on hurriedly, perceiving in this anecdote an element which might be interpreted to his own disadvantage— "mind you, he wouldn't have got in even if the King—God bless His Majesty—had been sponsoring him...I tell you what, we'll go and sit over by the window, where there's some air."

Carrying their drinks, they moved to the embrasure he had indicated and settled down there, Captain Watkyn with the relieved sigh of one who after long and tedious journeyings has returned home.

"Snug little place," he observed, looking about him. "Might be a bit quieter, though, mightn't it?"

Fen agreed that it might.

"Well, never mind," said Captain Watkyn consolatorily, as though it had been Fen who had complained. "You might be very much worse off, if I know anything about it...Well, now, sir, you must let me have your instructions."

"What," Fen asked, "has been happening so far?"

"A great deal," Captain Watkyn replied promptly. "A great deal has been happening. In the first place, I've induced ten people to nominate you—they're a job lot, but they're rate-payers, which is the only thing that matters. So that's settled.

And then, the posters and leaflets have arrived this morning from the printer. He's taken a devil of a time doing them, but that's all to the good."

"How is it all to the good? I don't see—"

"The point is, old boy," Captain Watkyn interrupted, "that you get quite an advantage by starting your campaign late. You acquire the charm of novelty. Start too early, and you'll find people get sick of seeing your silly face peering at them from the hoardings (no offence meant). Now, you're going to come down on them," he said, waxing suddenly picturesque, "like the Assyrian on whatever it was. They'll be bowled over. They won't have a chance to look about. Then along comes Polling Day, and you're in."

"Yes," said Fen dubiously. "I dare say that's so."

"You may depend on it, old boy. The old firm knows what it's doing, believe you me. Now then, we must get down to brass tacks. The posters have been distributed, and they'll be up by tomorrow."

"What is on them?"

"Well, your photograph, of course," Captain Watkyn replied dreamily. "And underneath that they say: 'Vote for Fen and a Brave New World.'"

"I scarcely think—"

"Now, I know what you're going to say." Captain Watkyn raised one finger monitorily. "I know just exactly what you're going to say. You're going to say that's exaggerated, and I agree, I'm with you entirely, make no mistake about that. But we've got to face it, old boy: these elections are all a lot of hocus-pocus from beginning to end. It's what people expect. It's what people want. And you won't get into Parliament by saying: 'Vote for Fen and a Slightly Better World If You're Lucky.'"

"Well, no, I suppose not...All right, then. What about the leaflets?"

"I have some here." Captain Watkyn groped in his pocket and produced a handful of printed matter, which he passed to

Fen. *"The Candidate Who Will Look After Your Interests"* it said on the outside.

Fen studied it bemusedly while Captain Watkyn went off to get another round of drinks.

"You'll like that, I know," Captain Watkyn said complacently on his return. "It's one of the best things in its line I've ever done."

"But all this...it isn't what I wrote to you."

"Well, no, not *exactly* what you wrote to me," Captain Watkyn admitted. "But you see, old boy, it's no use trying to stray away from the usual Independent line: you'll get nowhere if you do."

"But what *is* the usual Independent line?"

"Just Judging Every Issue On Its Own Merits: Freedom From the Party Caucus: that sort of thing."

"Oh. But look here: this says I advocate the abolition of capital punishment, and really, you know, I'm not at all sure that I do."

"My dear sir, it doesn't matter whether you do or not," said Captain Watkyn with candour. "You must rid yourself of the idea that you have to try and implement any of these promises once you're actually elected. The thing is to get votes, and with an Independent candidate you have to fill up election pamphlets with non-party issues like capital punishment, because the only thing you can say about major issues is that everything will be Judged On Its Own Merits."

"I see. Then when I make speeches I have to stick to these non-party things?"

"No, no," said Captain Watkyn patiently, "you mustn't on any account do that. You must talk a *great deal* about the major issues, but you must keep to pious aspirations, mainly." An idea occurred to him. "Let's have a test. Imagine I'm a heckler. I say: 'What about exports, eh? What about exports?' And your reply is—"

Fen considered for a moment and then said:

"Ah, I'm glad you asked that question, my friend, because it deals with one of the most important problems facing this country today—a problem, I should add, which can be only imperfectly solved by any of the rigid, prejudiced party policies.

"'What about exports?' you say. And I reply: 'What about imports?'

"Ladies and gentlemen, there is no need for me to talk down to you. Politics are a matter of common sense—and common sense is that sphere in which ordinary men and women excel. Apply that criterion to this question of exports; cut through the meaningless tangle of party verbiage with a clean, bright sword. And what do you find? You find that exports mean imports and imports mean exports. If we wish to import, we must export. If we wish to export, we must import. And the same applies to every other people, of whatever race or creed. The matter is as simple as that.

"'Simple,' did I say? Yes, but vitally important, too, as our friend so rightly suggests. All of us want to see England prosperous; all of us want to build for our children and our children's children a future free from the hideous threat of war. And I'm sure you won't consider it a selfish aspiration if I say that all of us would like to see a few years of that future ourselves. And why not? It's a great ideal we're fighting for, but it isn't an impossible ideal...

"Ladies and gentlemen, the world is at the cross-roads: we can go triumphantly forward—or we can relapse into barbarism and fear. And it is for you—every one of you—to choose which way we shall go.

"Well, sir, I think perhaps that answers your question. There may be some points I've missed, as the monkey said when he fell over the hedgehog..."

Captain Watkyn was professionally impressed.

"You're a natural, old boy," he said soberly. "Can you keep that sort of thing up?"

"Indefinitely," Fen assured him. "The command of *cliché* comes of having had a literary training."

"Then we're in the money," said Captain Watkyn. "Here, we must have another drink on that."

They had another drink, and Captain Watkyn, sighing contentedly, said:

"Well, I don't mind telling you now, Professor Fen, that I was a bit nervous at first about how you were going to turn out. I've had some queer customers to handle in my time, and sometimes it's been touch-and-go whether they could put a complete sentence together impromptu. Thank God we don't have to worry about *that*.

"Now let's map out a plan of campaign. My idea, in addition to the regulation meetings, is to make a separate appeal to each section of the community."

"In what way?"

"Well, I've been over the ground pretty thoroughly," said Captain Watkyn, "and I think I've got a fair notion of what we're up against. This is an easy constituency in a way, because it's completely apathetic: half the people won't vote at all, for anyone. And a good proportion of that half are the women. These country women tend to think the whole thing's a lot of idiotic humbug suited only to men, and I won't say," Captain Watkyn added handsomely, "that I think they're far wrong... Anyway, we don't have to appeal to the women so much as we should elsewhere, so you can tone down the brave-resourceful-queuing-housewife-and-mother angle."

"And that leaves what?"

"It leaves the farmers and farm-labourers, chiefly. Do you know anything about farming?"

"Nothing whatever."

"It's just as well, perhaps. Your best line with them will be to attack the Ministry of Agriculture, which they all detest. I'll try and collect some actual local cases of meddling for you to use, but you can always get on in the meanwhile with the usual man-on-the-spot-knows-a-sight-more-about-the-job-than-a-pack-of-Civil-Servants-in-Whitehall angle."

"I can manage that all right," said Fen. "Who else is there?"

"There's the Sanford Morvel crowd, mostly shopkeepers. The-small-trader-is-the-backbone-of-national-prosperity will do for them, only you'll have to remember that agriculture's the backbone of national prosperity, too."

"And everything else."

"Everything else that goes on *in this constituency*," Captain Watkyn amended. "Then there's Peek. Peek's not going to be too easy. Peek, between ourselves, is one of the most ruddy awful places I've ever come across in my life. The only thing I can think of that's likely to appeal to Peek is a sort of general prospect of getting something for nothing."

Fen felt whatever principles he had slipping finally and irretrievably into limbo before Captain Watkyn's determined and far-reaching doctrines of expediency.

"Is that the lot?" he asked weakly.

"There are still the professional people, upper middle class and so forth. Not many of them, but they tend to vote."

"And what tale do I spin them?"

Captain Watkyn seemed hurt.

"Look here, old boy, don't you go getting any wrong ideas about me. I know as well as you do what a grand thing democracy is. But the way I look at it is this. You're obviously the sort of clever, high-minded chap who ought to be in Parliament. Very well, then. But how are you going to get there? Answer: you've got to be elected.

"Now, these Sanford people don't know you as well as I do," Captain Watkyn pursued, with a confidence which their quarter-hour acquaintance did not seem to Fen entirely to justify, "and since they're mostly chronic imbeciles they're quite likely to elect some scoundrelly nitwit who'll help send the country to the dogs. Therefore they've got to be jollied along a bit—for their own good, d'you see?"

"As Plato remarked."

"As whatsit remarked, yes. Once you're elected, *then* your principles and so forth come into play. See what I mean?"

Fen, on the point of drawing attention to the well-known fact that means determine ends, came abruptly to the conclusion that the moment was inopportune, and subsided again.

"Yes, I see what you mean," he said reservedly.

"Then we're all set," said Captain Watkyn. "Now, today's Saturday. My idea is to concentrate all your meetings as close to Polling Day as possible. This afternoon, of course, there's the Nomination business in Sanford Morvel. Then tomorrow evening I've arranged for you to hold a kick-off meeting there after Church hours. On Monday morning you're going hunting—"

"I'm *what*?"

"Hunting, old boy. Cubbing, actually. There's a very keen hunt in these parts. Get you a lot of votes if you turn up."

"But I've never hunted in my life," said Fen. His knowledge of the subject was derived almost exclusively from Surtees and the *Irish Resident Magistrate*.

"That's all right," said Captain Watkyn easily. "You can ride, can't you?"

"In a way."

"Then don't worry, old boy. I'll be there to give you moral support. And I can easily get the loan of a couple of quiet nags."

"No," said Fen.

"If you went," Captain Watkyn urged, "it'd give you a lot of pull with a certain sort of people, because neither of the other candidates will be there. The Conservative man can't ride, and the Labour man daren't, for fear of offending *The New Statesman*...Just you think it over."

"No."

Unlike Oxford, Captain Watkyn had no time to waste on lost causes. "All right, then," he said resignedly, "we'll cut that out…Now, let's see. Most of the rest of the week you'll have to spend touring about to God-awful places like Peek, and talking at street corners. But of course, we'll hold a slap-up final meeting on the evening before Polling Day."

"That sounds satisfactory," Fen agreed. "And are there any people who are going to canvass for me?"

"Well, not yet," said Captain Watkyn. "There aren't actually any such people yet. Matter of fact, I tried to rope in the chaps who are nominating you, but they turned a bit nasty. Still, I shall find someone, never fear."

"And have I got a loudspeaker van?"

"Well, yes. It doesn't work very well, because it's rather an old one, but there's an electrician johnny in Sanford Morvel trying to fix it up."

"And a car?"

"I've seen to that, too," said Captain Watkyn. "We'll pick it up after the Nomination."

"And do we need a committee room? I dare say I could get a room here if necessary."

"Well, we haven't got a committee, have we, old boy? No, I think we'll dispense with that for the time being. No point in burdening ourselves with unnecessary expenses—the law only allows us a certain amount of money to play about with, you know…Now: is there anything else, I wonder?"

"What are the other candidates like?"

"Oh, they're not much," said Captain Watkyn with contempt. "The Conservative—chap called Strode—is a farm-labourer who's been to night classes. And Wither, the Labour man, is a big industrial magnate from somewhere up North. They've been chosen that way to try and make an appeal to the sort of people who aren't normally expected to vote for their parties. Of course, it won't make the slightest difference in the end, but it gives party H.Q. the illusion of being up-to-the-minute."

"Do you think I've got a chance of getting in?" Fen asked.

"Not a doubt of it, old boy," said Captain Watkyn heartily. "Think success: talk success. That's my motto, and always will be."

Fen eyed him rather coldly. "But apart from sales talk, I mean."

Captain Watkyn's cheerfulness abated slightly.

"Well, I don't know," he said. "In the normal way, to be quite candid, I should say you hadn't got a chance in a million. But politics are funny. They're like racing. Hundred-to-one outsiders romp home and leave all the experts gaping. So you needn't despair," said Captain Watkyn, resuming his more specious manner. "No need for despair at all. Now I'll tell you what: we'll drive in to Sanford Morvel for lunch, and then there'll be the nomination business, and after that you can back here to—" he gestured vaguely—"to prepare your mind and so forth…How about one for the road?"

CHAPTER SEVEN

So THEY HAD one for the road, and after Captain Watkyn had ascertained that Fen was provided with the cheque for his deposit, left the Inn. Captain Watkyn's car proved to be a rather old Bugatti sports model, and in it they set off for Sanford Morvel. The journey was without incident except when Captain Watkyn stopped beside a seedy-looking man who was shuffling along the road, gave him two pound notes, murmured: "Assyrian Lancer, Newmarket, 3.30," and drove on again. "Damn silly names these horses have," he observed to Fen.

Sanford Morvel looked as if it were trying to be a gracious, peaceful country town and failing very badly. Its main street was wide but vacant-seeming; its Town Hall was old but ugly; its shops and pubs and houses had uniformly succeeded in missing the great periods of English domestic architecture; its Church was squat and sullen. Fen and Captain Watkyn lunched on ill-cooked meat and tepid vegetables at the White Lion, a pretentious but comfortless hotel in the Market Square.

Afterwards they went to the Town Hall, where the deposit and the Nomination papers were given with due form to the Sheriff, and where Fen shook hands with Strode and Wither, neither of whom (since the occasion was not a public one) evinced much cordiality to him or to each other.

Following this ceremony, Fen was introduced by Captain Watkyn to the car he was to use, a lumbering old Morris no longer capable of doing more than twenty miles an hour. In it, having received a promise that Captain Watkyn would collect him in time for the meeting tomorrow night, he drove languidly back to Sanford Angelorum.

On the way he stopped the car in order to look at Sanford Hall. It was a large building, of the eighteenth century apparently, set well back from the road in extensive grounds and partly screened by trees. The sun shone brilliantly; the vista was quiet and unpeopled. Fen left the car, found an entrance to the grounds of the Hall and, undeterred by considerations of trespass, went through it.

Crossing a small coppice of beeches, he came on a curious scene.

By the side of a small stream, about thirty yards off, Diana stood talking to the young man in shabby tweeds with whom Fen had seen her earlier in the day, and whom in default of other evidence he identified as Lord Sanford. It was impossible to tell what the conversation was about, but it did not seem to be a particularly amicable one. Diana was gesticulating vehemently; her eyes flashed, and her mouth, when she spoke, was twisted at the corners with indignation. The young man seemed less angry than harassed; evidently he was on the defensive. Their voices came to Fen's ears, through the hot summer air, in weak spasms of uninflected sound.

But it was not the apparent quarrel which chiefly interested him. It was the presence among the beech trees of a watcher other than himself.

The fair-haired girl who called herself Jane Persimmons was partly hidden by one of the tree trunks, and the hand she had pressed against it was rigid, with the knuckles white. A narrow shaft of sunlight rested on her cheek, but her eyes were in shadow and unreadable. All Fen could tell was that what she saw interested her passionately. He thought, too, that she was not deliberately eavesdropping—that like himself she had come here accidentally, and not much before him at that. But the scene, for some reason, had gripped her, and until it was finished she was incapable of moving, whether she would or no.

Now, however, Diana and the young man were moving away, up towards the dower-house. Jane Persimmons stiffened and made a short indecisive movement as if to follow. Then she relaxed and turned slowly away.

And turning, she saw Fen.

It was easy for him to read what was in her mind. Principally, it was shame at being caught in a harmless but equivocal act; secondarily, it was a desperate resolve to try and appear natural, as though she had a right there.

She stumbled a little on a root; attempted to smile; stammered a conventional greeting; and then turned and half ran back through the coppice. More slowly, Fen followed.

Reaching the car, he found her waiting for him there, shifting her small, neat bag from hand to hand. She had decided, evidently, that the occurrence called for stronger measures than mere flight.

"I—I wanted to see the Hall," she said. "It's very beautiful, isn't it?"

At that moment she seemed very small and friendless, and Fen was touched. He smiled with reassuring charm.

"Delightful," he answered. "I was trespassing, too. Can I give you a lift back to the Inn?"

"N—no, thank you. I came out for a walk, and I shan't go back yet."

"Then I'll be seeing you later."

"Just—just a minute." She put out a hand to stop him. "I—Do you know Lord Sanford?"

"I'm afraid not."

"Oh!" She gave a little gasping laugh. "Well, I hope—I hope you won't tell him I've been spying on him."

"I shan't tell a soul," Fen assured her. "And you must do the same for me."

"That's a bargain, then," she said. And beneath the outward flippancy he knew that she was desperately in earnest.

"That's a bargain," he said seriously. "You're sure I can't take you anywhere?"

"No, really, thank you."

"Goodbye for now, then."

As he drove off, he saw in the driving-mirror that she stood looking after him until a bend in the road hid him from her. He wondered if he could have done more for her; she had seemed, somehow, so very much in need of help and advice. Better not offer those commodities, though, until he was asked for them...

And of one thing at least he was sure; whatever might have been her motives in watching Diana and Lord Sanford, this girl was incapable of a mean or a flagitious act.

He parked the car in the Inn yard alongside the non-doing pig, which was lying gracelessly on its side in what appeared to be a stupor. The total quietude of the Inn made it clear that Mr Beaver and his family had given up for the day and gone home. And Fen, yawning copiously, decided that the most agreeable thing to do now would be to lie on his bed and fall asleep; which accordingly he did. He was slightly troubled by a recurring dream in which Mr Judd, uttering American college cries, pursued a scantily clad Jacqueline in and out among the Doric columns of a Greek temple, but in spite of this inconclusive drama he awoke at seven in the evening feeling considerably refreshed.

Dinner he ate alone in the room where he had break-fasted, Myra informing him that neither of the other guests was booked to appear. This room evidently adjoined the bar, for he was able to hear the perennial argument going on within a few feet of him.

"She'm close-'auled, I tell 'ee."

"No, no, Fred, you'm proper mazed. See them? Them's 'er gaff-tops'ls.'

"Mizzen-tops'ls."

"Mizzen, gaff, 'tis all the bloody same."

"What I says is, 'er's runnin' before the wind."

"Look 'ere, see that ship at anchor, see? Now, if 'er was moored fore *and* aft, you wouldn't be able to see not which way the bloody wind was blowing. As 'tis, she's facin' out yards sea. An' that means—"

"But she is moored aft. You can see it. You can see the buoy."

"That's no buoy, Fred, that's just a drop o' bloody paint."

"I'm tellin' 'ee 'tes a buoy."

"Well, look 'ere now, if that brig's close-'auled, that means..."

The meal over, Fen settled down with some beer and a detective story, becoming so engrossed that it was not until nearly closing-time that a sudden outbreak of abnormal excitement in the bar restored him to consciousness of his surroundings. Reluctantly abandoning the heroine to the suspicious circumstances in which she had foolishly contrived to entangle herself, he went to see what was happening.

The commotion, he found, was centred in a pitiful-looking middle-aged man in gamekeeper's clothes, who had the air of one who has been suddenly and horribly sobered up in the middle of a gay carouse.

"'Ow was I to know it was 'im?" he kept saying. "'Ow was I to know?"

"Poor old Frank," said Myra. "He's afraid they're going to have him up for murder."

Fen asked to be told the cause of Frank's distress, and Myra embarked willingly on a narrative of characteristic raciness and gusto.

It appeared that the lunatic, still at large, had manifested himself again. Mother-naked as before, he had jumped out at a very ancient spinster called Miss Gibbons as she was walking home from an evening spent with a great-nephew and his wife at the other end of the village. In this emergency Miss Gibbons, however, had despite age and infirmity displayed a markedly aggressive spirit; of sterner stuff than Mrs Hennessy, she had seized the lunatic by the hair and shaken him ferociously to and fro until, recovering from his surprise, he had torn himself away and fled.

Thereupon Miss Gibbons had let out an eldritch shriek which brought half the village, including Constable Sly, to her assistance.

Constable Sly had at once taken charge. He had enlisted the help of Frank the gamekeeper, as being the possessor of firearms, and the two of them had set off in pursuit, Frank carrying a loaded revolver. They had traced the lunatic up onto the dingy nine-hole golf course which serves the neighbourhood, and had thought they saw him disappear into one of those huts which are erected on golf courses to shelter golfers from sudden showers; and Sly had instructed Frank to remain on guard outside while he, Sly, went in to make the capture.

As it happened, they had been mistaken, and the lunatic was not there; after a short search, therefore, Sly had emerged from the hut empty-handed. Unluckily, however, Frank the gamekeeper had spent the earlier part of the evening celebrating some undefined stroke of good fortune; and sighting Sly's unidentifiable form on its way out from the hut he had erroneously assumed that this was the lunatic, had levelled his revolver in an excess of alcoholic enthusiasm, and had shot Sly in the leg. Sly had been removed, in an unforgiving state of mind, to the hospital in Sanford Morvel, and Frank had proceeded to the Fish Inn, where he was now engaged in monotonous self-justification.

"...might 'a' knocked Will out," he was saying, "and 'a' bin escapin'. What I says is, Will oughter 'ave given me a sign, like. Whistled, or that. 'Ow was I to know it was 'im?"

However, there is always something pleasing to us—as La Rochefoucauld has remarked—in the misfortunes of others. The Inn's customers were rather ribald than sympathetic, and the luckless Frank had to endure a good deal of facetiousness, for which he compensated by drinking deeply at other people's expense. Presently Myra, tiring of his reiterated complaint, called time. By slow degrees the company dispersed. And Fen, who was by no means immune from the application of La Rochefoucauld's pejorative law, departed contentedly to bed, where he dreamed the whole night through about a naked lunatic pursuing Mr Judd in and out among the Doric columns of a Greek temple. Psycho-analytically (he decided later) it was an improvement on the afternoon's effort.

CHAPTER EIGHT

As ON THE previous morning, he was awakened promptly at seven by the onset of Mr Beaver's renovations. As punctually, that seraph-like vision which was Jacqueline brought in his tea. He arrived downstairs as the Church bell began ringing for eight o'clock Communion, and was moved by this Sabbath noise to attend the service. Only half a dozen others, it appeared, had succumbed to a like impulse, but he was pleased to see Jacqueline among them. The choir sang a four-square Victorian setting with conspicuous heartiness, and Fen, accustomed to the unobtrusive sleekness of Oxford liturgies, found his attention wandering. He examined the Rector, a substantial, sallow, mephitic-looking man of some sixty years who was named in the Church-porch notices as W. Scantling Mills. "'Dark Satanic mills,'" Fen thought. He walked back to the Inn with Jacqueline, who continued to preserve a contented and decorative silence.

The man who called himself Crawley was alone at the breakfast table, a pencil poised inactively over the *Observer* crossword. Seen at close range, he did not inspire much disquiet. His chin receded, his nose was long, his eyes were a guileless blue, his whole appearance mocked Fen's amorphous forebodings of criminality. And identification followed quickly; it had only eluded Fen so far for want of a proper look. The name explained itself, too.

"Bussy," said Fen.

Bussy returned the pencil to a pocket; it was a gesture of resignation. "Hullo, Fen," he said agreeably. "I was afraid I couldn't stave off this meeting much longer." He paused to consider the remark, separating its more offensive suggestion from its intended meaning. "That is to say," he elucidated painstakingly, "that for business reasons I should have preferred that we didn't meet. Personally, of course, I'm delighted. How are you, after all these years?"

"I'm well." Fen sat down, selected a spoon, and began delving into half a grapefruit. He eyed Bussy thoughtfully. "We can remain mere pub acquaintances if it suits you, you know. As I remember, you're in the C.I.D."

Bussy nodded. "Detective-Inspector, by the skin of my teeth."

"And actively engaged on something."

"Yes. More or less unofficially, I should add. I'm not supposed to be here. The local police would probably be very annoyed if they knew I was." This reflection seemed to gratify Bussy; he gave a low chuckle.

"I see." Fen gazed at him in mild perplexity. "But your disguise is very inappropriate. No one does any fishing here."

"As I've discovered. I was misled, in advance, by the name of this pub."

Fen poked earnestly at a segment of grapefruit which had been inadequately cut. "And other people besides yourself are acquainted with *Vanity Fair.*"

"No one has noticed that so far except yourself. But the point, Fen, is this. I'm the world's most incompetent actor. When I act, infants in arms perceive that I'm acting. So I was never specially perturbed at the thought that people would see I was not what I made myself out to be—that was inevitable, anyway."

"In that case, any sort of masquerade—"

"Would serve the purpose. The world might know that I wasn't what I appeared, but it still wouldn't know what I actually *was*, and that was all I needed."

Fen finished his grapefruit and rang a handbell. Myra produced obese, uncompromising sausages. They were silent until she went away again, Fen groping in his mind among the lees left by his undergraduate days. Bussy had been his contemporary; had read English; had nourished an unqualified enthusiasm for Thackeray; had—while Fen entered upon those devious courses which issue in Oxford Fellowship—selected subsequently, from some preference which remained impenetrable, to join the Metropolitan Police Force. And here he was. The reunion was rather casual than cordial, but then, they had never been greatly attached to one another.

Bussy, his eye on the closing door, said: "I'm afraid I must ask for your discretion. I shan't be here very much longer, but I want to remain incognito if possible."

"I shall say nothing." Fen reached for the toast. "I shall be too busy to gossip, in any case."

"But you're curious?"

"My dear chap, of course I am. Are you in a position to tell me why you're here?"

Taking a pipe from his pocket, Bussy separated it into several pieces and began poking about in them with a bedraggled gull's feather. In this prolonged and devout ritual of preparation Fen recalled, he had always indulged.

"I don't see why not," he said slowly. "Most of the facts you could get from the papers, anyway. Perhaps you have got them from the papers, already."

"Perhaps I have," Fen agreed. "But until you tell me to what they relate, I can scarcely be sure of it."

"A murder," said Bussy. "The murder of a woman called Mrs Lambert."

"A French lady," Fen suggested, "poisoned through the post?"

"So you have read about it."

Fen shook his head. "No, I've heard it referred to, that's all. I don't read about crime in the papers, because there's no space these days for details."

"But you yourself"—Bussy looked at him with some calculation—"have been involved in a certain number of investigations. Those two murders at Castrevenford, for instance."

"I solved them," said Fen, with the impregnable air of one who asserts that the earth is a globe.

"But all your cases have been rather *recherché*. I'm not sure that there's much for you in this. Or rather—"

Bussy paused, again in calculation, and Fen tapped the mustard spoon impatiently on the side of his plate. "The facts," he said balefully. "Unless, of course, the solution's already settled and obvious. Finished histories don't appeal to me greatly."

"I'll tell you this much." Bussy spoke, now, with rather more emphasis. "There's one curious aspect of the evidence which seems to me to point pretty directly to a certain conclusion." He paused, while Fen struggled to assimilate this uncommonly nebulous statement. "Only no one else seems to see it."

"Ah," said Fen reservedly.

"Yes, you're quite right to be sceptical," said Bussy, not without gloom. "I've wondered myself if I'm imagining things.

Of course, when I say that others don't see it, I don't mean that I've *expounded* it to them and they *still* don't see it.

"No."

"I just mean that it hasn't *occurred* to them. And that's what mystifies me, because to me it's so self-evident that I can't see why it hasn't occurred to them."

"It would be better," said Fen with commendable patience, "if we clothed these bones with a little flesh. My mind isn't at all adapted, at this hour of the day, to deciding why an undefined set of people confronted by an undefined set of facts should not have arrived at an undefined conclusion. It's altogether too metaphysical. Expound Mrs Lambert, please." He poured out coffee.

"All right." Bussy nodded, with a brisk movement substituting for the gull's feather a small pen-knife, with which he proceeded to scrape about inside the bowl of his pipe. "See if you see what I'm getting at."

He subjected the little room to a heavily professional scrutiny. The single sash window was open, but the table at which they sat was so near to it that no eavesdropper outside could hope to evade observation. The door was firmly shut. There were no places of concealment. The walls were admittedly thin, but the tireless labours of the Beaver *ménage* made it highly improbable that Bussy's words would be audible at more than a few inches from their source. Their sole companion was a Niobe who, tastefully framed in light oak, gazed anxiously down at them, apprehensive—it was possible to surmise—of a sudden assault on her virtue. Bussy frowned at her, ejected some species of filter from the depths of his pipe, fumbled among his clothing for a fresh one, and said:

"A fortnight ago—on the afternoon of August twenty-eighth to be exact—a woman living just outside Sanford Morvel was poisoned. She was married to an Englishman, a solicitor called Lambert, but she herself was French—or more accurately, half French and half Russian. Her father, a *bourgeois* of sorts, very sensibly got out of Russia during the Menshevik *régime*, and her mother was a dancer at the Opera.

"I needn't hold forth about them, because they haven't anything to do with the story. The point is that they both died when this girl—Andrée—was only fifteen, and left her penniless, with the result that she became a prostitute. I don't mean"—Bussy gestured perturbedly—"that she deliberately chose that unpleasant career. Of course, she *may* have done—it hasn't been possible to get any details—but from what I've heard about her character it seems to me much more likely that she was victimised. There are a good many ways in which that could happen to a pretty, poverty-stricken girl living on the *rive gauche*, and no doubt you can imagine them for yourself."

Fen, who had finished eating, concurred, with a kind of grunt, in this estimate of the more worldly capacities of his mind. He was anxious to encourage Bussy to leave as much unsaid as possible, since the neighbourhood's insect life, sun-drunk and at present percolating into the room in increasing numbers, promised considerable discomfort to anyone who was foolish enough to sit still for any length of time. Bluebottles were settling on the backs of his hands; a wasp, impersonally vehement, hovered at his ear; platoons of mosquitoes, in places so thick as to seem almost ectoplasmic, were performing a species of *Hexentanz* round his head. He blew cigarette smoke at them, which they seemed to enjoy, and grunted again, with enhanced emphasis.

"It's clear, in any case," said Bussy, "that she wanted to abandon that sort of life as soon as she got the chance, because she contrived somehow or other to save a bit of money and have tuition at a secretarial college. And eventually, at the age of nineteen, she got a job with a firm in the

Avenue Mozart—Demur et Cie—which hires out secretarial workers for short-term assignments and piece-work. It also makes, or at any rate made, a specialty of training one or two girls in English, so that visiting English business-men can employ them. You get rather higher wages in that job, and Andrée took it on. That was how she met Lambert."

Bussy began to reassemble his pipe. "Lambert isn't a business-man, of course," he resumed after a brief interval of manipulation. "He's a solicitor, as I said. But he has money of his own, so he doesn't practise nowadays. And as a matter of fact, he's always been more of an academic authority than a practical lawyer. Have you heard of Lambert on Company Law?"

"Vaguely," said Fen.

"That's the man. Anyway, he went to Paris to meet a lot of other experts on Company Law. Not my idea of a picnic—" Bussy stirred uneasily as he contemplated this uncouth occupational mafficking—"but I suppose it was his. The upshot of it was that while he was there he found he needed a secretary, and Demur's sent him Andrée. And the upshot of *that* was that he brought her back to England and married her."

Here Bossy paused prolongedly, mentally sorting the vagaries of the erotic instinct into some kind of plausible sequence; and Fen, who guessed what he was doing and who was not anxious to have the psychological inwardness of the union explained to him, took the opportunity to say:

"Yes, I can understand that. It's the sort of thing which happens more frequently than one imagines."

"Only in this case it was perhaps specially surprising." Bussy was not to be deterred by this ready acquiescence. "You'd understand that if you'd met Lambert, as I have. He's not only orthodox and conventional: he's *militantly* orthodox and conventional, with a particularly rigid code of honesty and honour and an air of moral severity which I must say is a bit daunting. And all that is very relevant to what happened a fortnight ago. The thing is, you see, that when he asked her to marry him Andrée didn't tell him about her seamy past. I dare say she ought to have done. But as far as I can gather she was genuinely in love with him and horribly afraid that if he knew she'd been on the streets he'd throw her out and refuse ever to see her again. So she kept silent, and I don't suppose anyone but a prig would blame her for that. After all, her past was a misfortune rather than a fault; she'd slaved to make herself respectable; and it would have been insanity to abandon the chance of real happiness and security for the sake of a Roman principle. I imagined that if he'd asked her she'd have told the truth. Only he didn't ask her.

"They were married in Sanford Morvel just before war broke out. Being a year or two above military age, Lambert got a job as one of the legal advisers to the Ministry of Supply, but it didn't disrupt his home life to any serious extent, and the marriage undoubtedly thrived. There was mutual sympathy and good sense as well as love. And until three weeks ago they were an almost ideally happy pair."

Fen's campaign against the incursion of insects had withered for lack of attention; by now he was a good deal interested in Bussy's narrative.

"I see what's coming," he said thoughtfully. "Blackmail."

"Exactly. Blackmail." Bussy examined his pipe, blew through it experimentally, and began with great deliberation to fill it from a sealskin pouch. "Sentimental claptrap about blackmail—'the meanest of crimes' and that sort of conventional jabber—I haven't normally much use for. If a man has committed a crime and got away with it, then I cannot see that another man who extorts money from him as the price of silence is one half as disgusting, morally, as a thug who savages an old woman in order to steal her life's savings. But where it's blackmail for a mere fault—and even more for a fault for which the wretched victim can't be held responsible—then, I agree, it's nauseating.

"And of course, that was the case with Mrs Lambert."

Brooding, Bussy stared out of the window. Beyond it were well-kept beds of vegetables; beyond them an orchard; at the far extremity of that, a thicket hedge with a small, decrepit wooden gate in it. And from hedge and gate a gentle slope of rough pasture mounted to the sky-line, with three thin birch trees—forgotten sentinels of a disbanded army—huddled together in isolation close to the top. It was a placid scene, but it seemed to heighten Bussy's indignation rather than to allay it; he thrust tobacco into his pipe with needless violence.

Fen, whose theory it was that flies may invariably be crushed by clapping one's hands together immediately above the place where they have settled attempted without success to do this.

"I suppose the business ran its normal course?" he ventured. "Final demands that were never final?"

"No," said Bussy irritably. "It didn't. And that's what makes it so peculiarly sickening. Everything pointed to an uncommonly happy ending, and then—

"But I'd better not anticipate. Here's what actually happened.

"Mrs Lambert got the usual sort of letter—this happened a bit less than a month ago—threatening to tell her husband that she'd been a prostitute, and circumstantial enough (it gave the address of a brothel where she'd lived in a street just off the Rue de Rennes) to convince her that the writer knew at first hand what he or she was talking about. I say 'he or she,' but it appears that Mrs Lambert never had any doubt that it was a man, and probably someone who'd once slept with her. I've seen the letter, and I can't make out how she deduced that from it, but I give you her opinion for what it's worth, and the probability is that she was right.

"Well, the sum demanded wasn't excessive, and she could lay hands on it without any difficulty; so she paid. Her husband, she knew, was fond of her, but she couldn't be sure how he'd take a revelation like that.

"But naturally, a second demand followed very rapidly. Mrs Lambert decided that that sort of thing couldn't be allowed to go on, and made up her mind to tell her husband all about herself and damn the consequences. She was amazed to find that he wasn't in the slightest perturbed— amazed, that is, until he told her that he'd known all along; that he'd known, in fact, even before he married her. He blamed her neither for her past nor for not mentioning it to him, and she realised then that this business wasn't going to make the smallest difference to their relationship; that they were going to be able to carry on as happily and as confidently as before."

At this point Bussy produced a new-fangled pocket lighter which smelled of ether, and applied it to his pipe. "Well, that was settled," he went on, "and they agreed to consult the local police. Lambert had to be away for two or three days, so his wife did the consulting alone. Twenty-four hours later, a box of chocolates came for her through the post. Probably she imagined they were from her husband— anyway she ate several of them unsuspiciously; but someone had injected strychnine into them, and within two hours she was dead."

He fell silent, inhaling deeply. A series of metallic crashes, accompanied by a hoarse shouting, came to their ears, suggestive in its ferocity of a piratical sea-fight with cutlasses. Fen moved restively in his chair.

"Did she speak before she died?" he asked.

Bussy shook his head. "No. She was alone in the house, and her body wasn't found until several hours after she was dead."

"And she didn't succeed in leaving any written message?"

"None." Bussy glanced at Fen with a certain respect. "I'm glad you see the point." ("I always do," Fen grumbled.) "If it was the blackmailer who sent those chocolates, then he must have had some particularly urgent reason for wanting her silenced; and that reason can only have been that she'd recognised him—someone out of her past who was living in the neighbourhood. So she might have left some indication of his identity. Only she didn't. When you're dying of strychnine, you're not capable of anything very much."

Fen considered. "Is it possible that the chocolates weren't sent by the blackmailer at all?"

"It's possible, yes," said Bussy grudgingly. "But as far as the investigations have gone, it's very unlikely. The husband, for various reasons with which I needn't bother you, is quite definitely out of it. And we haven't been able to unearth a shadow of motive for anyone else. It's a fair assumption that the blackmailer is also the poisoner."

"You said 'someone who was living in the neighbourhood.' "

"The blackmail letters were posted in Sanford Morvel; so were the chocolates. Beyond that, we haven't got any clue. The chocolates were in a small, flat container, and the poisoner was able to post them in a letter-box. So there's no lead there—as there would have been if he'd left them at the Post Office counter. The wrapping doesn't help. Nor do the letters. So far, the case has been a series of dead ends."

"And the mechanism for conveying the blackmail money?"

"Also a dead end. I can explain it, if you like," ("No, no," said Fen hastily.) "but it's a carefully contrived scheme, and there's nothing at all useful to be deduced from it."

"So the result of this extensive nescience," Fen observed, "is that Scotland Yard has been called in."

"Not at all." Bussy grinned, ingenuously sly. "Scotland Yard has *not* been called in."

"From the point of view of the public, you mean."

"From the point of view of anyone. The Chief Constable is relying on Wolfe, the local Superintendent. Neither of them knows I'm here."

"Is this, then,"—Fen stared at him rather blankly—"a kind of criminological holiday task?"

"No. It's Lambert's doing. Lambert is a friend of the Assistant Commissioner. Lambert doesn't believe that the local people are capable of dealing adequately with the matter of his wife's death. Lambert consequently asked the Assistant Commissioner to intervene. The Assistant Commissioner pointed out, very properly, that he couldn't do that unless the Chief Constable asked him to—or at least, not without provoking a lot of bad blood. But he did agree to compromise between friendship and professional ethics by sending me down incognito. So I'm here officially-unofficially as it were, and Lambert is the only person locally who knows who I am and what I'm doing. For the purposes of the record, I'm on leave, and any meddling I do is simply the result of personal inquisitiveness."

"I should have thought that in that position you would have been hamstrung from the start."

"Not quite. No, not quite. It's had certain positive advantages...But now"—Bussy's glance was definitely wary—"you've heard a brief outline of the facts. Have you made that obvious deduction I was talking about?"

"I've made one deduction which seems to me obvious," Fen replied cautiously.

"Well?"

"If the blackmailer is also the poisoner, with the motive you suggested—"

"Yes."

"And granted that Mrs Lambert's husband was away, so that she had no one but the police to confide in—"

"Again, yes."

In a few words Fen explained what he thought and Bussy sat back in his chair with a sigh of relief so heartfelt as to be almost a groan.

"Thank God," he said. "I was beginning to have doubts about my sanity. It *is* obvious, isn't it?—and yet as far as I know, no one else has thought of it."

"You've found nothing to militate against that theory?"

"No."

Fen was abnormally pensive. "It wouldn't stand by itself, of course," he said. "You'd need additional proof."

Bussy knocked out his pipe, returned it to his pocket, and got to his feet. The breakfast table had by now a crumby, congealed look; the insect battalions continued to riot light-heartedly in the air above it; a bar of shadow which had stolen across Niobe's milkmaid face had the effect of seeming to intensify her virtuous disquiet. Bussy glanced at her and then looked hurriedly away again, rather as a well-bred man might do who had happened on a girl undressing behind a rock.

"I've got additional proof," he said. "Or rather, I anticipate having it in a day or two."

Fen studied him a shade sombrely. "Be careful," he advised. "Your activities may have aroused suspicion, and a person who has risked one murder probably wouldn't mind risking a second. Does anyone else know of this—this evidence you're collecting?"

"Not yet. It isn't complete enough for a report."

Bussy wandered to the door. With his hand on the knob he said: "You needn't worry. No one is likely to catch me unawares, I can assure you of that...By the way, we'd better revert to the status of casual acquaintances."

Fen nodded.

"And you'll keep what I've said absolutely to yourself?"

"Of course."

"Good." Bussy smiled. "I must make a move now; there's a good deal to be done. I shall be glad to put this poisoning creature in the dock—and apart from that, it *might* mean promotion for me...Thanks for listening. Goodbye for the present." He waved a hand and was gone.

CHAPTER NINE

THAT EVENING FEN went to his first election meeting.

At the outset it did not seem likely to be a conspicuous success. The hall in Sanford Morvel which housed it was of that kind, peculiar to the English genius, whose heating is defective, whose lights illuminate only those parts which do not require illumination, whose windows are worked by an agglomeration of screws, rods and cog-wheels of which the motive power, a detachable handle, seems perennially to be mislaid—a hall, in brief, which the architect has designed to accommodate itself to almost any social activity from church bazaars to *The Mikado*, and which in consequence accommodates itself to none. A large gathering might have humanised it to some extent, but there was not, in this instance, a large gathering. Even Captain Watkyn was slightly taken aback by the number of empty chairs.

"Of course, old boy," he said *sotto voce* to Fen as they climbed onto the platform, "you haven't got to expect too much bang off. And Strode and Wither are both holding meetings, otherwise there'd be more people here. Still…"

The chairman, to Fen's surprise, proved to be Mr Judd—at the moment perceptibly a creature moving about in worlds not realised. Fen had mentioned his name to Captain Watkyn at their previous meeting, and Captain Watkyn had coaxed him, by a considerable expenditure of energy, into officiating on Fen's behalf. Viewing him now, Captain Watkyn was inclined to regret this step, for Mr Judd's demeanour and speech embodied panic and black melancholy in about equal proportions.

"I *hate* speaking in public," he kept muttering aggrievedly. "I *detest* speaking in public."

"Come, come," Fen muttered back. "I'm sure you'll do very well."

"I shall *not* do very well."

"I happened," Fen pursued with shameless untruth, "to mention to Jacqueline that you were going to introduce me, and she said I couldn't have found a better man."

"Did she?" said Mr Judd doubtfully. "Did she really say that?"

"Certainly she did. I gathered that she has a good deal of admiration for you." Fen paused fractionally to evolve fresh falsehoods. "Unluckily she couldn't get here tonight, but I promised to tell her everything you said and did. And—quite off the record, of course—she said that if I was pleased with the show you put up, it would go a long way towards confirming her own good opinion of you."

In a less flurried condition even Mr Judd would scarcely have swallowed this grossly implausible tale; but in the present circumstances his natural credulity was reinforced by the desire to clutch at any straw of consolation, and he brightened visibly.

"Well, I'll do the best I can," he conceded.

"Of course you will. And there's no need for you to go on for long."

In the event, however, this last inducement turned out to be singularly irrelevant. After a little initial clumsiness Mr Judd got quickly into his stride; and whereas earlier the problem had been to persuade him to start, the problem was now to persuade him to stop.

"Hence it is," he was saying after twenty minutes' uninterrupted magniloquence, "that we want—no, passionately and most urgently *need*—intelligent and disinterested men like our friend here to break and forever destroy the vicious circle of nepotism, jobbery and party conflict. And shall I tell you why it is in *this* constituency—this, and no other—that that great crusade must begin? The answer, ladies and gentlemen, is what we all know in our heart of hearts. And that answer is: because it is in our incomparable countryside that England's strength and wisdom and endurance reside not in the haste and waste of the great Wens"—Mr Judd was an assiduous reader of Cobbett—"but *here*, amid those fields and woods which have bred, and whose memory has sustained through every trial, every testing, our country's very greatest men; here in the English countryside that has endured for centuries, and shall for centuries endure."

Upon this resounding period Mr Judd paused for breath; and at last perceiving, or anyway decoding, the surreptitious signals which Captain Watkyn had been directing at him' for the past ten minutes, brought his speech with ill-concealed reluctance to a close, and sat down amid more cordial applause than either he or anyone else could previously have anticipated.

Fen followed with a speech which, if less Ciceronian and impassioned than Mr Judd's, was even more effective; and although its content does not bear summarising, it succeeded in evoking some semblance of positive enthusiasm in the thirty or forty people present. Lecturing at Oxford had trained Fen to fluency in public speaking (though admittedly this happy consummation is inconspicuous in the majority of dons). By the highest standards his oratory was not exceptional, but it was none the less several degrees superior to anything that Wither or Strode could manage, for Strode's mind worked slowly, so that his speeches were peppered with long intervals of dead silence while he considered what to say next; and Wither was prone to a facetiousness so abominable that even the electorate of Sanford—a district not renowned for delicacy of wit—felt it an affliction. Fen consequently started with a marked advantage over his opponents, and made so good an impression, even in the chilling circumstances of this first meeting, that for the first time Captain Watkyn began seriously to envisage the possibility of his being elected.

Such few questions as were asked, Fen answered with an appearance of great candour; and he was untroubled by heckling, since at this time the professional hecklers of the Labour and Conservative parties were respectively occupied at the Conservative and Labour meetings. The close of Fen's meeting consequently found everyone relatively gratified, and Mr Judd in a state of elation which bordered on incoherence. He fluttered about while Fen interviewed the canvassers whom Captain Watkyn had assembled in his cause, and insisted on returning to the Fish Inn to be present while his triumph was communicated to Jacqueline. It was perhaps fortunate that on arrival there they found Jacqueline absent and Myra alone behind the bar. And Mr Judd's disappointment, though great, proved possible to mitigate with cherry brandy and the vague assurance of a subsequent meeting.

Fen left him and went upstairs to change, for the evening's exertions had made him sticky and uncomfortable. He took his time over this, and was somewhat abashed, on his return, to find that the bar had closed, and that Mr Judd, relapsing after his brief interregnum of glory into a more normal diffidence, had gone home. Myra was still there, however, and he asked for beer.

"A pint, my dear?"

"Please. And have something yourself."

Fen drank largely, and was on the point of demanding news of the lunatic, and of Constable Sly's progress, when the door of the bar rattled as someone outside banged against it.

"Now, who the devil's that?" said Myra.

She crossed to the door and unbolted it. The non-doing pig came in. It looked dusty and fatigued, as though it had just completed a very long journey.

"My God, he's back," said Myra.

"Back?"

"I sold him this afternoon. He didn't want to go, I could see that. And now he's escaped from Farmer Lumley and come all the way home." Myra was evidently rather moved by this demonstration of fidelity. With the toe of her shoe she prodded the non-doing pig amicably in the ribs, at which it staggered visibly.

"Poor thing, he's worn out," she said with compassion.

Fen put some beer in an enamel basin for the pig, and after it had drunk some of this it turned and staggered out of the door again, and they could hear it making its way round to the Inn yard.

"He'll have to be taken back tomorrow, though," said Myra firmly.

Fen finished his own beer and decided to go to bed. In parting from Myra he asked about the lunatic.

"They haven't caught him," Myra said, "though they think he's still in the neighbourhood, because there's been food stolen from one of the cottages. They say he's got 'a madman's cunning,' which is their excuse for being too dim-witted to catch him…Good night, my dear. Sleep well."

❀ ❀ ❀

By the following morning it was apparent that Mr Beaver and his renovations were no longer confined to the room in which Fen had first encountered them. A loss of their original concentration and vehemence was compensated for by a great increase in scope, with the result that—although as yet half the Inn remained untouched—the clouds of plaster dust which emanated from the operation began to seem omnipresent. It was not easy, Fen found, to distinguish one member of the party from another. Basically, it was a family affair: Mr Beaver, his wife, and along with them two sons and two daughters all of whom looked about the same age—say seventeen. But its composition was spasmodically varied by the addition of employees from Mr Beaver's drapery business and of acquaintances whom Mr Beaver had cajoled by some means into volunteering for temporary service; and this, added to the family resemblances, the dirt which masked all their faces, and the general haggardness which resulted, no doubt, from repeated early rising and the unintermitted ingestion of powdered whitewash, did nothing to lessen Fen's confusion.

And if the identities of these people were inexplicable, their aims were even more so. In the intervals of spurring on his band, Mr Beaver was, it is true, to be seen peering intently at some kind of architectural plan. But Fen, who chanced to find this lying about and examined it at length, was unable to equate it at any point with what Mr Beaver was actually doing, and was forced to the conclusion that he intended to make a clean sweep of the whole interior of the Inn before attempting anything in the way of reconstruction. Partitions between rooms were pulled down, flooring was demolished, ceilings crumbled, doors were removed from their hinges and left lying about where the unwary might most readily fall over them. Fen's room, and indeed all of the upper storey, remained for the present inviolate, but Fen doubted if this immunity was likely to last very much longer, and in the meantime meals had to be transferred to a sort of boxroom upstairs, where the eating of them was a comfortless business. The noise increased hourly. Since the weather remained fine and warm, customers at the bar preferred to do their drinking outside, in the pleasant grounds of the Inn.

During the morning and the earlier part of the afternoon Fen was busy canvassing in Sanford Morvel, his efforts, though variously received, increasing rather than diminishing Captain Watkyn's hopes of a victorious outcome to the election. In the matter of personality, Fen was more generously endowed than either of his opponents; he could talk easily and amusingly to anyone, of whatever class or occupation, and this gift was not shared by Strode, who got on well enough with the lower orders but was tongue-tied in the presence of anyone having an income of more than five hundred a year, or by Wither, who was effusive with the monied classes but offensively bluff with everyone else. A certain unease regarding Fen's candidature was already being felt at Labour and Conservative party headquarters. Neither had put an outstanding candidate into the field, partly because the election was not likely to be a political portent, occurring as it did in one of the brief hiatuses between the succession of domestic crises of that year, and partly because both parties regarded the outcome as a certain Conservative victory. Fen's late appearance on the scene had consequently taken them unawares, and now they were beginning to wish they had put up representatives more formidable than either Strode or Wither. However, it was, as Captain Watkyn observed, too late for them to do anything about it now that nomination day was over.

"And mark my words, old boy," he added, "the personal touch is going to be devilish important. Where there's political apathy it always is—in fact, it's the only thing that'll induce some people to vote at all."

Further support for Fen came from an unexpected quarter, namely, the editor of *The Sanford Advertiser* and *Peek Gazette*, whose offices Fen and Captain Watkyn visited in Sanford Morvel High Street. It transpired that this ancient but vigorous person, whose name was Gamage, had early in his journalistic career been successfully defended on an indictment for seditious libel by Fen's father, that learned if unaccountable barrister whose eccentricities are still remembered in the Inns of Court; and that in view of this notable service he was prepared to give Fen every assistance in his power.

"That's a stroke of luck, old boy," said Captain Watkyn as they left the office. "Mind you, we mustn't expect too much from it—no good counting our chickens before they're hatched—but it'll help to keep you in the public eye, and that's half the battle." He rubbed his hands together gleefully. "I tell you what, we'll have a drink on that."

Surveying it at large, Fen concluded that Captain Watkyn's organisation was on the whole very commendable, considering the unnaturally short notice he had had. Its principal defect lay in the continued unworkability of the loudspeaker van, which according to the reports of those who were labouring at it, and whom they visited about tea-time, was lacking in numerous essential parts.

"It's a ruddy scandal, that's what it is," said Captain Watkyn indignantly. "I'm not sure we couldn't bring an action for false pretences. What's the matter with this funny-looking terminal here? Damn the thing, it's given me an electric shock."

They left the electrician's, and Captain Watkyn, who clearly regarded a quasi-maternal solicitude as part of the duties for which he was being paid, advised Fen to return to the Fish Inn and rest there for the remainder of the day. "Mustn't overdo it," he said. "We want you fresh and lively for the final round." Fen accepted the advice readily enough; the buttonholing of recalcitrant voters, he had found, made heavy demands on one's reserves of nervous energy. He drove staidly back into Sanford Angelorum.

CHAPTER TEN

THE INN, HOWEVER, had not recovered from its habitual post-meridian inertia, and promised little in the way of entertainment. For a short time Fen prowled unquietly about it, avid of diversion or company to expunge from his mind the cloying after-taste of the day's routine affability. But he found nothing and no one, and presently a vestige of physical energy prompted him out of doors again. The sun was already westering, its fires refracted now and kinder to the eye; along the horizon the distant woods lay like a narrow roll of brown smoke; across a sky of Antwerp blue streamed shrilling hordes of unidentifiable birds. Fen paused in the back garden of the Inn and contemplated the operations of Nature a shade grimly. Then he set off on a walk.

It was an hour before he returned. Breasting the far side of the rise behind the Inn, his eye was caught by the lean apparition of Bussy—striding, from another angle of the compass, towards the same objective as himself. A moment more, and Bussy had seen him, had swerved, was moving with purposeful rapidity in his direction. They met by the three slim birch trees.

"I hadn't hoped to find you so easily." Breathing heavily, Bussy nodded his approval of the workings of chance. "Fen, I need help. You must help me. There's a small element of risk, I'm afraid, but you won't mind that."

Fen studied him, diagnosed a wholly conscienceless zeal, and sighed resignedly. Self-respect obliged him to concur in Bussy's facile assumption of his indifference to risk, but he did so without enthusiasm. "No," he said. "No, I shan't mind that."

"Good." Bussy dismissed the issue from his mind without exhibiting a sign of gratitude. "It's to do with this Lambert affair, of course. Something I can't manage single-handed. I can't give you the details now, I'm afraid, because I've got to catch a train."

Fen was surprised. "You're leaving?"

"To all appearance, yes. I want it to be thought that I've returned to London. But after dark I shall sneak back again, and you must meet me. I can explain the position then."

"And where," Fen asked, "do you propose spending the night?"

"In the open."

"That will be cold and disagreeable," said Fen practically. "You ought to find a shelter of some kind—if you're proposing to sleep, that is."

"All right." Bussy gestured impatiently. "No doubt a haystack or a barn—"

"Or you might try one of the huts on the golf course."

"Whatever you say." Clearly the topic held no interest for Bussy. "That would certainly have the advantage of providing a *locus in quo* for our meeting."

"And the time?"

"Let's say midnight. I shall almost certainly be back by then, but if I'm not, wait for me."

"Yes. I suggest the hut at the fourth green." Fen's walk had familiarised him with the topography of the course. "It's reasonably commodious."

"That will do," said Bussy. Then a new thought occurred to him. "Of course, Fen, you realise," he added considerately, "that you're in no way obliged to undertake this."

Fen opened his mouth to make some reassuring reply, but Bussy, who patently regarded his declaration as the merest formality, gave him no opportunity to do so. "That's settled, then," he said. "I shall look forward to having your cooperation." He could no more conceive of a refusal, Fen reflected, than a fanatical gardener can conceive of an affirmative answer to the question "Are you bored?" when conducting a guest on a tour of the flower-beds. It was inevitable, no doubt, that men with missions should display a certain *brusquerie*...

The Church clock struck six, and Bussy's determination gave place with some abruptness to anxiety. "My God, I must be off," he said. "I haven't had a chance to pack yet. I'll see you, then, at midnight."

"One moment. Are you telling anyone else about this—this manoeuvre? The local police, for instance?"

"No. Certainly not. And I rely on your keeping it strictly to yourself."

"Yes, I'll do that all right."

Bussy nodded, and with this much farewell turned and made off down the slope towards the Inn, absorbed, it was to be presumed, in the details of his scheming. For perhaps half a minute Fen stood watching him; then—but more slowly—followed. Single-mindedness, he reflected, is always obscurely ludicrous—and he smiled. But the smile faded on his recollecting that he was now committed to an indistinct and probably tiresome nocturnal labour; one, moreover, which had been characterised as involving "an element of risk." Risk is no doubt tolerable at the time of undergoing it, when the blood is impregnated with adrenalin; in prospect, however, and with its nature wholly undefined, it is conspicuously lacking in charm. Fen reached the Inn in a rather dreary state of mind.

Bussy had long since disappeared from sight; by now he was probably in the act of packing or of paying his bill. Skirting the back of the Inn, Fen was vaguely aware of a car's being driven away in the direction of Sanford Morvel, of quick, light footsteps receding along the village street, of the rumbling approach of some heavy vehicle and the blaring vehemence of its horn. But the impact of these things was on the remote periphery of his mind, and the shout of warning, the short, choked scream, the sudden skidding swerve, were held tranced for long seconds at that periphery before, with a sinking heart, he returned to full consciousness of his surroundings and knew them for what they were. Then he ran—ran across the Inn yard and out into the road.

A hundred yards along, it curved sharply. On the right, as you stood with your back to Sanford Morvel, was a high, blank wall of umber brick, screening the Inn from approaching traffic. And there was no pavement—only a fringe of grass and nettles less than a foot's breadth wide…Given these conditions, an accident was likely enough, and this accident had apparently been a bad one. The lorry, stationary now but with its engine still pulsing, stood diagonally across the road; the sprawled, motionless figure of Jane Persimmons lay almost beneath its wheels; and around her, as Fen ran up, there hovered the driver of the lorry, a middle-aged village woman and an old man, their faces a painter's allegory of mingled indecision and shock.

Fen knelt beside the girl, felt for her heart; it was beating still, though faintly and irregularly. He glanced swiftly, appraisingly, at the dark blood ebbing out through her tangled hair, at the gashed lower lip, at the dirt-smeared pallor of her face, at the bag which lay near her outstretched hand, its contents—a lace-edged handkerchief, a latchkey, a powder compact and lipstick, a cheap cigarette case, a book of matches—half spilled into the dust. Then he straightened up, made a split-second assessment of the relative intelligence of the three people confronting him, and said to the lorry driver:

"Go in at the door on this side of the pub. In a little office, just inside on the left, there's a telephone. Get an ambulance. Say it's either concussion or a basal fracture of the skull. And if they're going to be any use, they'll have to be quick about it."

The man—he was young, Fen saw, and trembling and on the verge of nausea—hesitated fractionally, then nodded and ran heavily towards the Inn. And again Fen knelt beside Jane Persimmons, his fingers testing the bone from ankle to cervix. On the body, he found, there was no palpable injury except bruises—though internal haemorrhage remained a possibility... He frowned, perplexed. The girl's condition was consonant enough with the *nature* of the accident; what problem there was lay in its *circumstances*. The approach of the lorry had been by no means noiseless, and it had hooted, prolongedly...

Above his head, the woman spoke—timidly and in low tones. "I dunno if 'ee'd like to bring the poor maid in my 'ouse, sir. I'd 'elp 'ee carry 'er there."

Fen smiled rather wanly and shook his head. "She mustn't be moved, I'm afraid." He stood up, brushing disjointedly at the knees of his trousers. "There's nothing that can be done for her until the ambulance arrives."

The woman looked down at the pretty, pathetic, blood-stained face with a compassion too full to admit of mere morbid inquisitiveness, and sighed noisily, shifting a half-empty washing-basket mechanically from one arm to the other. But she was not unnerved, Fen thought, as the driver had been. Unimaginative, probably; and for that reason a reliable witness. "You saw the accident?" he asked.

She had. Disposing damp clothes on a line in the garden, she had seen Jane emerge from the Inn yard and had watched her steadily as, preoccupied and walking fast, she came up the road. Undeniably the lorry had hooted; and until she was almost at the corner, Jane had kept well in to the side of the road. But then she had turned her head to look back at the Inn, and so doing had walked straight out into the middle of the road. "I shouted at 'er," the woman concluded. "But it didn't do no good. And the lorry swerved, but that didn't do no good, neither. So there it was."

"There was no one near her when it happened? She couldn't have been jostled or pushed, that is?"

The woman stared. "Oh, no, sir, she were quite alone. No one else except me Dad 'ere in sight."

"And you're certain the driver didn't run into her deliberately?"

She was shocked, antagonised. "That's a nice question!" she ejaculated indignantly. "Course he didn't, poor lad! Why'd 'e do a terrible thing like that?" And she removed herself two or three paces from the moral leprosy which had made the enquiry, eyeing it militantly and with overt distrust.

At this point the victim of Fen's imputation returned; an ambulance, he reported, was on the way. His account of what had happened amply confirmed the woman's; so also—though more inchoately—did Dad's. And there could be no possible doubt, Fen concluded, that the thing had been a genuine accident. Whence, then, his own scepticism? Well, the girl had been preoccupied; but brooding does not inevitably result in immolation—as witness the continuing survival of one of Fen's Oxford colleagues, whose perilous habit it was to perambulate the streets engrossed in a book. To him the senses continued to make their reports, and by some esoteric mechanism to deliver them at the very centre of the intelligence whenever his preservation required it. So also, presumably, with this girl. Only in her case the delivery had for once not been made, the alarm had not sounded. She must have heard the lorry and yet have remained totally oblivious to it.

The interval of waiting seemed interminable. The driver sat on the running-board of the lorry and smoked, fretful at inaction, his eyes fixed miserably on the body of the unconscious girl; the woman stared defensively at Fen, anticipating—it was possible to suppose—some further enormity; the old man retired behind his garden wall and weeded, pausing from time to time to peer vacantly in the direction from which the ambulance was expected. A few pedestrians stopped, gaped, proffered futile advice, passed soberly on. Presently Diana's taxi drove up to the Inn, and Diana, emerging from it, hurried up to them.

"Oh, Lord," she said to Fen. "This looks nasty. Is there anything I can do?"

"I don't think so, thanks. I'd ask you to drive her to the hospital, only I daren't take the risk of moving her."

"Concussion?"

"That or a fracture."

Diana grimaced. "Sounds bad." She picked up the handbag, restoring its contents to it, and laid it on the grass verge. "Do you know anything about her? Who she is, or—or what she's doing here?"

The question, Fen thought, was a little sudden. "No," he said. "No, I'm afraid not."

"Well, there's rather an odd thing about her."

"And that is?"

But Diana was looking at her watch. "I'll tell you later," she said equably. "If there's nothing I can do, I'd better go, because I'm supposed to be taking someone called Crawley to catch the 6.42, and it'll be a miracle if we make it...By the way, I hear your meetings are rather good."

"They are enthralling," said Fen complacently.

"I shall go to one and heckle you." She smiled, turned, and ran athletically back to the car.

Burdened with luggage, Bussy came out of the Inn as she reached it. He glanced at the forlorn group along the road and seemed to ask a question. The reply clearly reassured him, for he nodded briskly and plunged into the car. It backed, turned, and was gone. Not more than a minute afterwards the ambulance came.

The doctor and attendants had neither time nor words to waste; they stowed the girl away with rapid efficiency and drove off, leaving in their wake no more potent consolation than the fact that she still lived. With aggravating deliberation, a policeman who had accompanied them recorded names, addresses, statements. He rode back in the lorry to Sanford Morvel, and Fen retired to the Inn.

He found Myra alone in the bar—which already, at the encroaching threat of renovation, seemed dilapidated and sullen; just so, Fen thought, must the House of Usher have looked prior to its wholesale submersion, or Shiel's nightmare copper mansion on the island of Vaila...Myra, it proved, was still in ignorance of what had happened, having been down in the cellar at the time of the accident.

"Poor kid!" she said compassionately. "She wasn't much more than a kid, really...You know, since she came here I've had the impression something was *worrying* her. She seemed to be fretting, like, and nervous."

"Yes, I thought so, too."

"I suppose the police'll be getting in touch with her people?"

"I imagine so," said Fen.

Half an hour later there was a telephone call from the hospital at Sanford Morvel, requesting Jane Persimmons' address; and about nine o'clock Superintendent Wolfe, of the Sanford Morvel Constabulary, appeared at the Inn. He was a burly, clean-shaven man who exhibited less consciousness of the dignity of his office than is common in the police force. When he had looked at Jane's room, he conversed affably, over a drink, with Fen.

"Our trouble is," he said, "that the Nottingham address she gives in the register is the address of a boarding-house. I've rung them up, but she's only been staying there a month, and they have no idea whether or not there are any relatives alive. No doubt there's someone we ought to communicate with, but I'm damned if I can find out who."

"Then there were no letters in her pockets or her bag?"

"None. A diary without any entries was all I could find. It has the usual page for personalia, and the usual heading: 'In case of accident communicate immediately with.' But she's filled it in: 'the nearest hospital,' which shows a certain sense of humour but isn't useful."

"And nothing in her room?"

"Nothing. I've never come across anyone so completely devoid of papers. There's this, of course." Wolfe indicated a small, rectangular box of black steel which he carried under his arm. "But it's locked, and I can't find a key that fits it—which is odd—and I doubt if I'm justified in breaking it open. Still, I may hear something from the Nottingham police; they're going to go through her belongings there...You don't happen to know why she was visiting this neighbourhood, do you?"

Fen shook his head. "I've no idea."

"Nor has anyone." Wolfe finished his drink. "Well, I'd better be getting back. Glad to have met you."

"Before you go, tell me what the doctors think about her."

"Concussion. And they're not sure yet which way the cat will jump. She's still unconscious, of course, and probably will be for a day or two. Nasty business—and not less nasty because it was obviously her own fault...Well, well." Wolfe nodded amiably and departed.

Fen sought out Myra. He would be late returning to the Inn that night, he said—or possibly he might stay with friends and not return at all.

"Well, I'll give you a key, my dear," she said, "and then you can come in at the side door as late as you like. Jackie and me'll be late, too—we're going to a dance."

"Enjoy yourself."

"And you, my dear," said Myra. "Give her my love," she added pleasantly.

"Unluckily it isn't that," Fen said. "Duty, not romance. How is Samuel?"

"He was in again this evening. Offered me a couple of eggs, on a Condition."

Fen was shocked. "Two eggs? That's a very poor tender. Herod offered Salome a hundred white peacocks. Two eggs I should be inclined to regard as insulting."

"Yes I suppose it is, now you mention it." Evidently this aspect of the matter had not previously occurred to Myra. "Small eggs, too. More like a bantam's eggs, they were."

"Next time I should stand out for a hundred white peacocks. Or for beryls and chrysolites and sardonyx and chalcedony."

"Or John the Baptist's head on a charger," Myra supplied efficiently. "I shall stand out, anyway...You know what he says about his wife? 'She'm cold,' he says, 'she'm cold as a dead weasel.'"

"Poor fellow." Fen shook his head in commiseration. "Well, a pair of bantam's eggs aren't likely to buy him much consolation." Receiving the key, he retired upstairs and dozed fitfully on his bed until half past eleven.

❊ ❊ ❊

A quarter of an hour later he left the Inn. The moon, almost at its full, bloomed amid a million stars. *The eternal silences of those infinite spaces*, Pascal's hypothetized agnostic had remarked, *terrify me*; which meant, presumably, that they did not terrify Pascal. And where the interstellar immensities were concerned, Fen reflected, Christians certainly had the best of it. Mathematicians might adumbrate their billions and their myriads, *libertins* might tremble in contemplation of them; the Christian, secure in a cosmology which dismissed them as irrelevance, was at liberty to regard the multitudes of remote suns as having been designed with no graver purpose than to solace his eye on such nocturnal rambles as this; at liberty to think of them as seraphic peepholes in the floor of heaven, or (more vividly) as patines of bright gold... "*Now lies the Earth all Danaë to the stars*," Fen murmured inwardly—and thereupon abandoned theopathy and fell to considering the derivations of poetry. *Patines of bright gold. But the bright gold, with Danaë. Danaë to the stars.* Professionally meditating the possible genesis of Tennyson's line, he stalked silently through the kitchen garden and the orchard and out on to the slope behind the Inn.

The three birch trees might have been steeped in rime; and as Fen came in sight of the woods, he saw that they, too, lay in a tarn of silver light. A white owl flew low across the moon, its silhouette knife-clear, a field-mouse clutched in its beak; a few yards nearer the woods, and he heard the inebriate singing of nightingales. *A forest of nightingales*; it was not improbable that within it lurked, in the person of the lunatic, a Circe's son—his intentions less subtle than those of Comus, but basically, no doubt, the same. Moreover, there breathed somewhere beneath this moon the murderer of Mrs. Lambert, so that, as regarded nightingales, Eliot's "stiff dishonoured shroud" was probably more apposite than Williams' oblique and lovely vision...In the golf-course shelter Bussy, his mind impervious to nocturnal magic, would be brooding on strychnine—and at this dismal reflection Fen momentarily halted. Cat-like, he cherished the hours of darkness; it was his view that they belonged, inviolately, to Faëry and to high adventure; and although it was to be presumed that adventure of some sort awaited him, he suspected that it would prove to be laborious and squalid rather than swift and ennobling. It was with reluctance that, resisting the lure of renegation, he entered the wood.

No encounter, priapian, homicidal or other, enlivened his passage across it. At the far side he climbed a stile and was on the golf course, amid a thicket of gorse whose butter-gold flowers were blanched now and obscurely sinister. The fairway of the third lay before him, and he walked down to the green. The fourth, he recalled, was a short hole which involved driving across a bramble-filled dip with steep sides. Into this he scrambled, and out again at the other side. The green, and the hut, lay before him. And there might—he halted, apprehensive—be someone moving hurriedly and silently away from it: in this deceptive light, though, it was difficult to be sure... Walking more swiftly, he came to the hut and stood at the entrance; inside, a fragmentary orange glow, itself visible, yet had no power to illumine the pitch blackness.

"Bussy!" Fen whispered.

And now there was movement—movement and a prolonged, toneless, hollow suspiration. Fen snatched a torch from his pocket and switched it on. The light fell on glazed eyes, on the glittering haft of a knife which projected from Bussy's mangled throat. Bussy's mouth moved, attempting speech; there came again that vacant, useless exhalation of breath; blood choked him; finger-nails scrabbled convulsively on wood.

After that, silence.

CHAPTER ELEVEN

At FIVE O'CLOCK on the following afternoon—which was the Tuesday—Superintendent Wolfe of the Sanford Morvel police and Detective-Inspector Humbleby of the Criminal Investigation Department, New Scotland Yard, called on Fen at the Fish Inn.

At the margin of the Inn's most substantial lawn there stood a large iron roller, about the size of those which are employed in flattening cricket patches. Its handle was propped, at an angle of some forty-five degrees, against the trunk of a beech tree, and Fen had discovered that, with the addition of cushions to ward off the metallic chill, it could be made into a tolerably comfortable easy-chair. Here he reclined in hieratic state, somnolently fretting. The sun, dropping inexorably towards the west, had left him in shadow—and he eyed it as balefully as if the cosmic mechanism had been contrived solely with a view to inconveniencing him. It would have been reasonable to expect—he reflected—that an election campaign would consume all one's available energies, that it would offer one a little of the fabled toil and excitement of ideological conflict. It was in this faith, certainly, that he had embarked on his four-day-old political career. By now, however, reasonable expectation was in full retreat, a victim of uncompromising fact. Anything less exciting than the Sanford by-election could scarcely be envisaged—and the blame for this lay not with the candidates or with their agents, but with the Sanford electors. To woo them politically was like attempting to discuss the binomial theorem with a broom; they were simply not susceptible to advances of that particular kind. Like fairy gold, or like those satanic houris which tempted the hermits of the Thebaid, they vanished at a touch, and were no more seen. In remarking that "a good many" of them were politically apathetic, Captain Watkyn had grossly understated the position—as, indeed, he had himself come to discover. For in exchanging guarded courtesies with his Labour and Conservative opposite numbers, he had learned that their candidates were hamstrung in exactly the same way as was Fen, that their meetings were scarcely better attended than Fen's had been on the previous Sunday, and that since meetings and canvassing were so patently barren of results, they proposed to indulge in these activities only at the minimum level required by professional decency...

Canvassing; Fen frowned. That morning he had canvassed in Peek, and a more conspicuous waste of energy it was impossible to imagine. Admittedly Peek was not characterised, as was Sanford Morvel, by spiritual vacuity; but it was notorious as a flourishing Black Market centre, and its surreptitious hawking of whisky and illegally slaughtered pork seemed to engross it to the exclusion of all other interests. Confronted by one whose mission was unconnected with illicit purchase or sale, Peek's only discernible reaction was a kind of embarrassed surprise—just such an emotion, Fen thought, as might be displayed by a genteel young woman who has accidentally overheard an improper anecdote.

He shifted to a more comfortable position and rear-ranged his cushions. The thwarting nature of his business in Sanford Angelorum would be just tolerable, he felt, if it did not so effectually interfere with matters of more liberal interest, such as the study of the various people he had met, and of the problems involved in the killing of Bussy and Mrs Lambert. Aggravatingly, he found himself in the position of a man who, weighing the merits of one entertainment against those of another, has chosen not only wrongly but also quite irrevocably. And it was little consolation to reflect that the civic indifference of the local populace would leave him a good deal of leisure to meddle in extraneous matters; sooner or later, at some crux, he would be dragged away to a street corner and obliged to descant on the various moral and economic backbones of this multitudinously vertebrate constituency...

Looking up, he perceived the approach of Wolfe and of Humbleby. With Wolfe he had had further talk, over Bussy's stiffening body, on the previous night; and at Humbleby's identity it was easy enough to guess. By this time the nature of Bussy's business in the neighbourhood must certainly have been revealed, and it was reasonable to envisage a certain tension between the Chief Constable of the county and the Assistant Commissioner at New Scotland Yard. But such tension—if it existed—was not echoed in the relations of Humbleby and Wolfe, which were clearly quite amicable. Humbleby—a neat, elderly, mild-looking man with a round red face and a grey Homburg hat tilted forward over his eyes—was introduced to Fen and expressed a courteous gratification; he peered about him, seeking chairs, and on seeing none squatted on the grass beside the roller. Wolfe imitated him. The tableau thus contrived was faintly absurd, Fen thought, suggesting as it did a lotus-eating oriental monarch receiving in audience the emissaries of an American oil company.

"Well, well." Humbleby glanced up at Fen in civil appraisal. "I'm very glad to find that you're not busy, very glad indeed. We've come—as of course you realise—to talk about poor Bussy's death."

"A damnable business," said Wolfe moodily. "You'd think a rural district like this would be peaceful enough, wouldn't you? But it's not two months since I was transferred to this Division, and already I've had to contend with a case of blackmail, a case of embezzlement, an escaped lunatic, a thoroughly nasty road accident and two murders, let alone petty larceny, Black Market and casual drunks...It might be Chicago."

"Difficult," said Humbleby perfunctorily; he did not seem much impressed by this catalogue of flagitious acts. "Difficult, no doubt...However, we'd better get down to our business."

"Which is—" Wolfe plucked a daisy and stared absently at it—"to ask you, Professor Fen, what you were doing on the golf course at midnight last night. I ought to have had that explained at the time, but in the commotion it was forgotten...You might," he prompted considerately, "have been taking a walk."

"But I wasn't." Feeling his recumbent attitude to be in some way discourteous, Fen straightened up. "I went there, by previous arrangement, to meet Bussy."

"Indeed." Humbleby's habitual mildness of utterance stiffened on the word. "Perhaps you would explain—"

"The way of it was this," said Fen. And he recounted the substance of his two interviews with Bussy—though for reasons of his own he omitted any reference to that oddity in the circumstances of Mrs Lambert's murder which both he and Bussy had observed. "So I arrived at the *rendez-vous* punctually," he concluded. "And there is the possibility that I saw the murderer escape—unless, that is, I was deluded by shadows."

"I think it's very likely that you *did* see the murderer escape." Humbleby nodded. "The police surgeon has confirmed a point which was already obvious enough—namely, that Bussy cannot possibly have lived for more than a couple of minutes after that knife was driven into his neck. If only you'd been five minutes earlier..." Then he gestured impatiently. "Still, it doesn't do to think of such things. In that variety of 'if' there is *no* virtue."

For a moment they were all silent, considering the implications of Fen's recital. Smoke curled lazily from one of the Inn's chimneys. Upon that slope where, twenty-four hours before, Fen had last spoken to Bussy, a sheep appeared, the vanguard of others which soon dotted the turf like fragments of dingy cotton-wool. And presently Humbleby said:

"Of course there's a motive there. Granted that Bussy had obtained, or was on the point of obtaining, evidence that would hang Mrs Lambert's murderer, then that murderer's only possible chance of safety would lie in killing him."

"A sound hypothesis," said Wolfe. "The only trouble with it is that as far as I can see we don't need a motive."

"Not need a motive?" Fen was startled.

"The indications," Wolfe explained, "are that it was Elphinstone who knifed Bussy."

"*Elphinstone?*"

"The lunatic. He was apparently camping in the hut for the night. It's the first real trace of him that we've found."

"But I didn't gather he was homicidal.'

"The actions of lunatics," said Humbleby a little testily, "are not predictable—and the forms of lunacy are not adequately understood. The doctors *say*, of course, that they can tell whether any given lunatic is liable to kill or not, but the plain fact is that they can do nothing of the sort. Moreover, Elphinstone's—as I learned from Dr Boysenberry this morning—is a complex and unclassifiable case; the second adjective meaning, I take it, that no one has the faintest notion what caused his madness, what will cure it, or what his reactions to any particular set of circumstances are likely to be. So I see nothing inherently improbable in the supposition that he killed Bussy."

"But with a powerful *rational* motive existing," Fen pointed out, "that supposition ought to be exhaustively tested."

"I agree entirely. And we might do well to discuss the point immediately." Humbleby paused, considering how best to approach it. "There's the possibility, of course, that Mrs Lambert's murderer came upon Bussy quite accidentally. But at such a time and place that's very unlikely, and for all practical purposes we can dismiss it. Then there's the possibility that Mrs Lambert's murderer—"

"Whom we might," Wolfe suggested, "call X."

"X, if trite, will be much more convenient," Humbleby assented briskly. "Where was I, now? Ah, yes. There's the possibility that X followed Bussy to the hut. And that I find quite incredible. Bussy must have been very much on the alert for that sort of thing, and it's *only* possible to tail a man undetectably so long as he has no suspicion that you're there. If Bussy had been followed, he would have known it. And if he had known it, he would certainly not have been taken unawares—the more so since he was carrying a gun."

"And that," said Fen from the empyrean, "leaves us with no other alternative than to suppose that X knew in advance that Bussy was coming to the hut, and waited for him there."

"As you say. And this is where you can help us. *Could* our X, or for that matter anyone else, have known of the *rendez-vous*?"

"No, he could not." Fen spoke very definitely. "In the first place, Bussy wouldn't have told anyone—he was emphatic about that. In the second place, I didn't tell anyone. And in the third place, the conversation during which we fixed the hour and the locale, though it could have been *overlooked*—from the guest-rooms in the Inn, for example—couldn't conceivably have been over*heard*. I made sure of that at the time. We were speaking in low tones, and there wasn't any possible hiding-place within earshot."

"All of which," said Wolfe, "would seem to settle it that X did not murder Bussy. And, incidentally, it's perhaps worth adding that even if Bussy did inform some third person of the *rendez-vous*, that very fact would have made him approach the hut with caution, a thing he evidently didn't do...We have to exclude X, then."

"Unless"—Humbleby was faintly jocose—"we choose to identify X with Professor Fen...However, if that identification were correct, it would hardly be in Professor Fen's interest to insist that no one but Bussy and himself could have known of the appointment." And Humbleby, with what he evidently imagined to be great good-humour, leered.

"*I* didn't kill the man," said Fen rather coldly. "But I should like to know why you've concluded that the lunatic did."

"Well, it's like this." Humbleby ceased leering abruptly, and frowned instead. "There is, in the first place, the small camp-fire which was still smouldering just inside the hut. You saw it, I think?"

"Yes. From the amount of ash surrounding it, I calculated it hadn't been alight for much more than an hour."

"That," said Humbleby cautiously, "is as it may be...But the point I'm coming to is this: embedded in the heart of the fire was a pair of rimless pince-nez which Dr Boysenberry has identified as those which were stolen from his office—and stolen, beyond all question, by the lunatic—at the time of the escape. In the absence of contradictory evidence it's therefore reasonable to deduce that it was the lunatic who made the fire."

"Quite so," said Fen. "But he might easily have abandoned his camp, and gone elsewhere, some time before the murder took place."

"Yes. But over against that we must set the fact that he almost certainly stole the knife with which the murder was committed. You may still argue, of course, that he left it lying about and that someone else then picked it up and used it on Bussy, but that, I think, would be rather far-fetched."

"Certainly it would," Fen agreed. "But tell me about the knife."

"It was pinched yesterday evening," said Wolfe, "from the house of a man called Judd, who writes detective stories. It's a Pathan knife, incidentally—not that that matters. Anyway, Judd and his housekeeper were out all evening, and someone— presumably the lunatic—broke in through a window, pinched the knife and a tin of American ham—"

"Which, by the way, was found empty near Bussy's body," Humbleby interrupted.

"—and left behind him," said Wolfe in conclusion, "a signature."

Fen was interested. "A signature? Do you mean his name?"

"No, not that. It was some words scrawled in red paint on the kitchen wall: *Down with Taft.*"

"Down with *what*?"

"With Taft," said Wolfe, chuckling. "Taft, you see, was a candidate for the American Presidency in 1912."

"I still," said Fen, "entirely fail to understand—"

"Well, well, I'm not surprised." Here Wolfe laughed very heartily, therefore provoking Humbleby to gaze at him with overt displeasure. "And I certainly wouldn't have understood it but for the fact that Boysenberry supplied the police with a certain amount of information about Elphinstone at the time he got away from the asylum. Apparently Elphinstone is periodically convinced that he's Woodrow Wilson."

"Ah." Fen was at once enlightened. "And Taft was one of Wilson's opponents in the 1912 election. So at the time when Elphinstone broke into Judd's house he was presumably, in the character of Wilson, rehearsing the fevers of 1912."

"So one supposes," said Humbleby, nodding. "And that, in summary, is the case against Elphinstone. Not *absolutely* conclusive—but then, it's very rare to find a case that is."

"There's one thing you haven't mentioned," said Fen. "And that is fingerprints. If Elphinstone killed Bussy, his prints must surely be on the handle of the knife."

Wolfe shook his head; the raising of this issue seemed to depress him. "They aren't, though. Nor are there any prints anywhere in Judd's house."

"Then doesn't that mean—"

"It doesn't mean anything in particular. You see, in addition to imagining he's Wilson, Elphinstone has a fixation about *gloves*. He *likes* gloves, and wears them whenever possible, regardless of the weather."

Fen frowned. "But he doesn't, you know. I caught a glimpse of him when I was on the way here from the station, and he wasn't wearing gloves then."

"Ah, I'd forgotten you'd seen him. But he was nude then, wasn't he?"

"Except for the pince-nez, yes."

"Dr Boysenberry has told us," said Humbleby with decided gloom, "that the nudity-fixation and the glove-fixation never occur simultaneously. But the glove-fixation and the Wilson-fixation almost always do...I often think," he added peevishly, "that the diagnoses of lunacy sound nearly as insane as the lunacy itself. Anyway, the provable fact remains that Elphinstone delights in wearing gloves. So the lack of prints doesn't at all militate against his having killed Bussy."

The sun was perceptibly lower now, and a breeze was stirring among the leaves. Again there was a silence—and this time it was Fen who eventually broke it.

"The inquest," he said. "When is it to be?"

"Tomorrow, as things stand. And the funeral on Thursday."

"And you'll be taking the line that Elphinstone killed him?"

Humbleby shrugged. "What other line is there to take? No doubt it's convenient for Mrs Lambert's murderer that Bussy should die at this particular moment; but the evidence, as you've heard, definitely singles out Elphinstone as the one responsible."

"What I can't make out," said Wolfe irritably, "is where Elphinstone *is*. The whole district's been combed for him, but until last night there hasn't been a sign of him anywhere. And now he's disappeared *again*."

"You'll have to find him now." Humbleby spoke soberly. "Or else there'll be a general panic."

"Well, we're having in men from another Division," said Wolfe, "and I couldn't be more pleased. I can tell you, my resources have been strained to the limit just recently...Oh yes, we'll find him all right. In a day or two the whole place will be seething with coppers."

Fen stirred uneasily on his regal eminence. "Did you go through Bussy's pockets?" he asked. "And look at his luggage?"

"We did," Humbleby answered. "And found nothing to the purpose. Whatever views he may have had about Mrs Lambert's murder, he evidently didn't write them down. So as regards that we're as much in the dark as ever, unless"—he glanced up to Fen—"you have any notion of what he was planning to do."

"None whatever, I'm afraid," said Fen truthfully. "I was to have heard about it when I met him at the hut. I take it"—he peered down at Wolfe—"that the Lambert investigation hasn't produced any results so far."

"None. I was going to ask the Chief Constable to call in the Yard in any case—and now Humbleby's here I shall be only too glad to hand the whole depressing business over to him."

"Thanks," Humbleby said. "It sounds an alluring prospect."

"There's just one other thing." The mood of catechism had not yet left Fen. "How did Bussy cover his tracks in doubling back here?"

"We're still not entirely sure." It was Wolfe who replied. "We know he took a London ticket at the station here, and we know he changed on to the London train at Sanford Morvel. After that it gets vague, but we think he slipped off the train at Wythendale, pinched a bike in the town, rode it to Sanford Condover, abandoned it there, and walked the rest of the way to the golf course."

"And his luggage?"

"He put it all in the guard's van and left it to go on to Paddington." Humbleby stood up, brushing grass and earth from the seat of his trousers; and as he did so the Church clock struck six. "Time's hurrying chariot," he murmured. "Unluckily it drives us towards something less agreeable than the complaisance of a coy mistress; it drives us—to descend to the rather squalid facts—towards a conference with the Chief Constable. If we're to be punctual, Wolfe, we must go."

"I agree," said Wolfe; and he also got to his feet. "Well, thanks for your help, Professor Fen. I'm afraid we shall want you at the inquest tomorrow."

"I was resigned to that," said Fen.

"It may assist your election campaign. Or there again—" Wolfe became pensive—"it may not. Still..."

He paused, and a look of amazement appeared on his face.

"What on earth," he demanded in a different tone, "is that?"

CHAPTER TWELVE

For some time now a distorted noise had been approaching the vicinity of the Inn. All three of them had heard it, without, however, pausing in their conversation to consider what it might be. Now, merging as it was into distinct utterance, it could no longer be ignored—and in another moment its source came sluggishly into view. This was a loud-speaker van, moving along uncertainly in third gear, and driven by a middle-aged lady whose unbending and ferocious preoccupation with the task suggested little previous experience of it; all about the van were pasted posters advertising the merits and integrity of Gervase Fen; and from the quadrifoliate loud-speaker on its roof there issued, horribly amplified, the voice of Captain Watkyn.

"VOTE FOR FEN," it said, "THE CANDIDATE WHO is this ruddy thing still working old boy well what were you making faces for then oh I see WHO WILL PROTECT YOUR INTERESTS AGAINST CLASS DISCRIMINATION AND FACTIONAL STRIFE BY WHICH I MEAN THE LABOUR

AND CONSERVATIVE GANGS THE CANDIDATE WHO WILL JUDGE EACH AND EVERY ISSUE ON ITS OWN MERITS AND WHO WILL..."

With intolerable slowness the sound receded up the village street, leaving a trail of hysterically barking dogs in its wake. Fen stared after it in great embarrassment. "I think," he said thoughtfully, "that I may have to put a stop to that sort of thing."

"Ah, well, it's all part of the game, no doubt." Humbleby spoke with patent disingenuousness. "We shall see you, then, at Sanford Morvel Town Hall tomorrow afternoon."

"Two-thirty, to be exact," Wolfe supplied; then a new thought occurred to him. "About the Persimmons girl..."

"Oh, yes," said Fen. "How is she?"

"Worse, I'm afraid. They don't think she'll last much longer. And I haven't been able to find a trace of any relatives, so—the poor kid will die alone...I suppose..." Wolfe frowned suddenly—and a moment later relaxed again. "Lord, no; I'm getting murders on the brain."

"It was certainly an accident, if that's what you're getting at."

"Oh, yes, I've no doubt of it, really. Still, I wish I'd seen it happen—and if I'd stayed two minutes longer I should have done."

Fen was surprised. "I didn't realise you were here," he said. "I suppose it was your car I heard driving away."

"Probably. I had to come over and investigate some busy-body's complaint about drinking out of hours. The girl actually spoke to me as I was leaving—she'd lost her Personal Points, or something, and wanted to know—"

"All this may be very absorbing," Humbleby interrupted with impatience, "but really, Wolfe, we must be moving."

"Yes," said Wolfe obediently. "Sorry... Till tomorrow, then."

Fen watched them as they strode off across the lawn—Humbleby small and dapper, Wolfe large and decidedly imposing. For a few minutes he remained where he was, brooding over the facts which the interview had brought forth. Then he sighed, clambered down from the roller, collected his cushions and headed for the Inn.

The cushions belonged in the bar; and the task of replacing them was enlivened by an acrimonious discussion which was raging there when Fen entered—a discussion which involved Jacqueline, Myra, a louring youth and a buxom village girl whose health and vitality illumined a frame that was Renoiresque in the outspokenness of its contours. Apart from them, the bar was empty.

"I'm not gettin' mixed up with no police," the louring youth was saying doggedly across a half-pint of mild. "What I says is, once they got yer, they got yer. I'm not gettin' mixed up with no police."

Myra was indignant. "And what about justice, Harry Hitchin? You don't think about that, do you? Here's a poor devil been horribly murdered, and you and Olive saw the man as did it, and all you do about it is sit there on your bottoms saying you're not going to get mixed up with the police. Well, I know what's going to happen to you. You're going to get yourselves thrown in gaol for being accessories after the fact, you mark my words." And at this point Myra became aware of Fen's presence. "If you don't believe me, you just ask that gentleman there."

Harry Hitchin and Olive turned to look at Fen, and Olive emitted a little shriek.

"That's 'im," she said, pointing dramatically. "That's one of 'em."

"Of course it is." Myra was disgusted. "It was Professor Fen who found the body."

"I'm not getting mixed up with no police," Harry Hitchin repeated apprehensively. "Not me, I'm not."

"What is all this?" Fen demanded.

"Go on, Harry," Myra urged. "You tell him about it. He's not the police."

" 'Ow 'm I to know that? It's a trap, that's what it is."

"You had better"—Fen spoke with Rhadamanthine severity—"tell me everything you know. Otherwise it's the lock-up for both of you." They stared at him with antagonism. "The calaboose," he added for full measure. "The Big House. I'll have a small whisky, please, Myra."

A muttered conference ensued between Olive and Harry Hitchin. Fen received his whisky and contemplated them grimly as he drank it. Presently Harry said reluctantly: "Well, we don't mind you knowin' of it."

"That's very generous, I'm sure. What did you see, where, and when?"

"It were last evenin'." Harry gulped beer in an attempt to refresh his jaded nerves. "We was in the gorse by fourth green."

"The gorse. Surely, in the *gorse*, you can't have been—"

"We was mollocking," said Harry with distinct satisfaction. "She'm a rare un for mollocking, is Olive."

Olive appeared gratified by this tribute. "Me Grammer," she remarked, "me Grammer allus says: 'When oats be cutting, maids be riggish.'"

"Your grandmother is clearly a depraved old woman... What time did you arrive there?"

" 'Twere near eleven," said Olive; the moral defeat of her paramour seemed to have fanned into life whatever sparks of common sense she possessed, and she took up the tale with some zest. "And moon were almost full. Me Grammer she says: 'When moon be full, lads'll be wenchin'.'"

This repository of erotic love, Fen foresaw, was likely to keep the point of the recital almost indefinitely in abeyance. "For heaven's sake," he said, "leave your grandmother out of it."

"She'm a rare un," Harry interpolated—feeling, perhaps, that he must not lose the conversational initiative altogether. "A rare un, is Olive's Grammer."

"Evidently she is. But at the moment I'm trying to get at what, if anything, you both saw."

"You just keep your trap shut, 'Arry 'Itchin," said Olive with sudden ferocity, "or you'll be after fashin' the genulman." And here she grinned enticingly at Fen and hitched her skirt several inches above the knee, possibly with a view to repairing whatever social damage Harry's indiscretion might have done. " 'Twere full moon, then," she resumed, "an' we weren't 'ardly settled in gorse afore we sees a Stealthy Form goin' into 'ut."

"A Stealthy Form? Does that mean someone you can't identify?"

Olive nodded. "We was too far off to see 'oo 'twas."

"But anyway, it wasn't a woman?"

"Might 'a' bin a woman," said Olive. "Woman in trousers, that's to say. Some girls, they wears trousers, and you sees their fat 'ips fair bustin' out of 'em." She paused, contemplating this indelicate vision with evident pleasure. "Might 'a' bin a man, though," she admitted after some thought.

Fen sighed. "It didn't occur to you that it was the lunatic?"

This possibility had clearly not struck Olive before. "Lor', no!" she exclaimed, wide-eyed. "We would 'a' up and runned if we'd thought 'twere the daftie. This Form, see, 'e lit a fire in 'ut, an' I says to 'Arry, 'T is nowt but a tramp,' I says, and 'Arry, 'e says—"

"I says, 'Shut up talking,'" Harry observed. "'Shut up talkin',' I says." He felt, obviously, that the masterfulness of this injunction might serve to elevate him, in Fen's eyes, from the disrepute into which he had fallen.

"So we watches the 'ut for near on an hour," Olive went on, ignoring the interruption, "an' then, near midnight, along comes another chap, a lean un, lookin' back over 'is shoulder as 'e walks. An' 'e goes into 'ut, and then there's a kind o' noise. "

"A kind of noise?"

"Like a scuffle. An' 'Arry, 'e says, 'Lor',' 'e says, 'they'm fightin'. We'd better get out of 'ere, quick.'" Wincing at this pitiless comment on his manhood, Harry mumbled something indistinguishable. "But afore we could move," Olive continued with rising excitement, "out comes the first chap, and off 'e goes. An' then a minute after, you comes along an' looks in the 'ut an' 'urries away again. An' after that," she concluded with simplicity, "we goes off an' finishes our lovin' elsewhere."

" 'T weren't none of our business," said Harry defensively.

Fen sighed anew. "And you don't think you'd recognise this first man if you saw him again?"

"No," said Olive promptly. " 'E didn't come the way you and the lean un came, so we couldn't site 'im proper."

"You said you watched the hut between the time the first man arrived and the time the second man arrived. Did anyone—*anyone*—enter or leave the hut during that hour?"

Olive shook her head, emphatically. "We'd be certain to 'a' seen if anyone 'ad."

"But surely, if you were—ah—mollocking, your attention—"

"We'd 'a' seen," Olive reiterated with great certainty. "We'd 'a' seen, 'cos 'Arry's afeared me Dad'll be after 'im with a knife, an' 'e knows it if anyone's comin' towards 'im, even so much as a mile orf."

"I ain't afeared o' your Dad," said Harry pettishly. "Don't you go sayin' I'm afeared o' your Dad."

"That you are, 'Arry 'Itchin." Olive repudiated this slur on her veraciousness with vigor. "That you are. Why, what about the time—"

Fen intervened hurriedly. "Yes, well, never mind that now," he said. "The point is that your story's extremely important, and must be told to the police."

"Don't want to get mixed up with no police," Harry muttered. But now Olive rounded on him with considerable savagery.

"You'll do what I says," she informed him uncompromisingly. "An' what I says is, we go to the police, like the genulman tells us to."

At this, the poor remnants of Harry's self-assurance vanished like smoke before a gale. "Ur," he assented feebly.

"And I think you'd better do it straight away." His point gained, Fen became more genial. "Can either of you drive a car?"

"Ur," said Harry with dawning interest.

"Well, mine is round in the yard, and you can drive to Sanford Morvel police station in it if you like."

"Ur," said Harry eagerly.

"But be sure to bring it back in good time. I'm not providing it for you to mollock in half the night."

"Olive's Grammer," Harry remarked, "she allus says..."

"'When swallows be leaving, girls be conceiving,'" said Fen. "Will you kindly finish your drinks and go?"

They obeyed, departing hand in hand. Fen watched in silence as with a horrid grinding of gears they set off to face their ordeal. Then he ordered another whisky—this time a large one.

"What a couple," said Myra resignedly. "Daft as they come."

A small spate of customers entered the bar. Myra and Jacqueline served them. And Fen, perched on a stool, brooded. If Olive and Harry were telling the truth—and he saw no reason for supposing that they were not—then apart from Bussy and himself only one person, the murderer, had been at the hut on the previous night; which meant that the hypothesis of Elphinstone's having camped, decamped and been replaced by the rational X was no longer tenable. Either the murderer had been X, or he had been Elphinstone. And he must—Fen argued—have been Elphinstone, for the simple reason that by no possible means could X have known that Bussy was due to appear at the hut. And yet...Fen shook his head; a coincidence so thoroughly convenient for the murderer of Mrs Lambert surely deserved to be probed further. But in what direction was one to look? It was conceivable, he decided after a good deal of thought, that in a detailed knowledge of Elphinstone's lunacy some discrepancy might be found—as, for instance, that he abhorred tinned ham...And that necessitated an interview with the person in charge of the asylum at Sanford Hall. What was the name? Boysenberry. Fen finished his drink and went to the telephone.

CHAPTER THIRTEEN

SANFORD HALL, VIEWED in the morning radi-
ance of that continuing summer, was discreet rather than
arrogant, demure rather than impressive—and this in spite of
its considerable dimensions. Approaching it, at eleven o'clock
on the Wednesday, Fen saw that it lay along the crown of
the hill like an elegant toy, its carefully spaced sash windows
tactful and unobtrusive, its main door solid and dignified,
its plain chimney stacks neatly massed against the porcelain
sky. It spoke—to those capable of interpreting such wordless
messages—of the spacious and dignified days in which, Anne
being on the throne and Marlborough away at the wars, it had
been built; and to fill it with lunatics, Fen thought, argued
an aesthetic obtuseness rare even in a government official...
And yet, on further reflection, it was possible to modify this
opinion; for it was likely, after all, that the architect would have
preferred to have his lovely design associated with the often
cheerful irresponsibility of madmen rather than with the fitful
bureaucratic zeal of some meddlesome Ministry.

The permitted outlay for care of the gardens must have been small, since apparently it served for little more than to keep the lawns and paths tidy. And there was, Fen noted, no apparent provision for safely immuring the patients—nothing, that is, in the way of barbed wire or palisades. Nor, indeed, was there any sign of patients, except where, a good way off, a white-coated attendant was wheeling a wrapped motionless figure about in a bath chair. The Hall seemed asleep—and the impression of drowsiness was enhanced rather than disturbed by the thin tones of a portable gramophone which seeped from somewhere in the interior.

Fen came to the main door and, since it stood open, walked in. A porter, who but for the lack of both coat and cap might have been said to be uniformed, was sprawled on a kitchen chair in the hall. At Fen's entry he looked up from a sporting paper and asked without enthusiasm to be told Fen's business.

"I have an appointment," said Fen, "to see Dr Boysenberry."

The porter was clearly relieved at not being required to grapple with any affair more complicated than this. "Keep straight on," he said affably, "first corridor on your left, second door on your right." Then he retired again into his paper. "Wily Wilkie," he read out to himself. "Filomela; Fiddle-de-dee, ten to one."

Fen left him, and by following his instructions came to a door upon which was a brass plate bearing the inscription A. C. BOYSENBERRY, M.A., M.D., F.R.C.S. The sound of the gramophone proceeded from behind it. *"I think that I shall never see,"* sang the gramophone, *"a poem lovely as a Tree."* Fen knocked. There was no answer. He knocked again. There was again no answer. Tiring of the delay, he opened the door and went in.

The room in which he found himself was enormous, so large, indeed, as to be almost certainly the Hall's ballroom.

And its vastness was accentuated by the fact that only one remote corner of it was furnished at all—so that the effect was of a minute encampment in a gigantic desert. Far away across an expanse of polished floor Fen could see a flat-topped desk, with a telephone, a gramophone and a litter of papers on it. In front of the desk was an elaborately bedizened *pouf*; behind it sat a man whose greying hair was disordered and whose pince-nez hung askew on the bridge of his nose; behind him stood a very small book-case containing about five books; above this hung a signed photograph of the man at the desk; to the left of the photograph was a stupendous metal filing-cabinet with a typewriter and a pile of gramophone records perched on top. And there was nothing else in the room whatever.

His footsteps echoing noisily around him, Fen walked across to the desk; and as he came near it, the grey-haired man raised a finger to his lips, and pointed to the gramophone, in a pantomimic demand for silence. Fen began to experience misgivings; it seemed to him likely that he was confronted with one of Boysenberry's patients rather than with Boysenberry himself. Life imitates literature with doggish fidelity, and in literature such situations were common enough…Moreover, the grey-haired man's first remark, after the record was finished and he had taken it off, was not encouraging. "Are you," he enquired, "fond of ballads?"

"Well, no," said Fen cautiously. "I don't think I can say that I am."

"Well, I am. And the one we've just been hearing is a particular favourite of mine. '*Trees*' it's called. Do you know, I don't think I've ever come across a lovelier poem than '*Trees*.'"

"Indeed."

"*Poems are made,*" said the man, "*by fools like me, but only God can make a tree…*Mind you, in view of recent laboratory experiments the last part of the statement isn't strictly true, but still, it's a very fine sentiment, very fine."

"Are you Dr Boysenberry?" Fen asked doubtfully.

"Yes, yes, of course," said Boysenberry. "Naturally I am... And that particular recording of it is outstandingly excellent. Also, there's 'Passing By' on the other side."

"Unlike the Good Samaritan."

"That's not so satisfactory, though: one of these modernistic things with funny chords..." And here Boysenberry, at last mindful of the duties of hospitality, put the record reluctantly aside. "Well, do sit down," he said. "It will have to be the *pouf*, I'm afraid. We've been here for three years, but even now the Ministry of Works hasn't let us have a quarter of the furniture we need."

"And your office," said Fen reservedly, "is unusually large."

"It's a damned barn, that's what it is. You'd think in a building the size of this I could find a decent office, wouldn't you? But when all the patients and staff have been accommodated, this is practically the only thing that's left. I wanted to have it divided up into several smaller rooms, but they wouldn't let me. Said it had been designed by some famous man and was very beautiful." Boysenberry stared about him with unconcealed distaste. "Grinning Gibbon or some such name."

Fen sat down on the *pouf* and offered him a cigarette.

"Thanks," he said, taking it. "Well, now, perhaps you wouldn't mind stating your business."

"I telephoned to you," said Fen. "Yesterday evening."

"Ah, yes, of course. I made a note of it at the time." Boysenberry rummaged half-heartedly among the papers on his desk, but without, apparently, discovering anything to the purpose. "Perhaps you'd be so good as to repeat—"

"I've come," said Fen, "to ask for some information about Elphinstone."

Boysenberry's manner altered visibly; he became frigid. "It is quite impossible," he said icily, "for me to communicate confidential facts of that nature to any unauthorised person, Mr—er—"

"Fen."

"Mr Fen. You are, I take it, a journalist."

"On the contrary," said Fen. "I am the Oxford Professor of English Language and Literature."

And as Boysenberry assimilated this intelligence, his attitude underwent another rapid and remarkable change. He fluttered his hands agitatedly; his mouth widened in a rictus which was seemingly intended to convey the greatest possible cordiality. "Dear me," he said. "How extremely foolish of me...*Professor Fen. Of course.* This is a very great privilege indeed...What will you have been thinking of me, I wonder?" And he idiotically tittered.

The motives underlying this sudden change of front were by no means clear to Fen. "Very understandable," he murmured inconsequently. "Very understandable indeed."

"And our meeting like this the more delightful," said Boysenberry, "in that by Christmas we may *perhaps* be more closely associated."

Fen, on the point of denying all charm to such a prospect, restrained himself in the interests of his errand and said "Ah" instead.

"You don't quite catch my meaning, I suspect." Boysenberry continued to radiate a strenuous and determined good-humour. "But you will be aware, of course, that the Oxford Chair of Abnormal Psychology is to filled shortly?"

Not being aware of any such thing, Fen said "Ah" again.

"Well, I," Boysenberry continued modestly, "am applying for the job—by which I mean, of course, the position."

"Then I must wish you the best of luck," Fen responded with as much heartiness as he could muster.

"Ah, but it's not all a matter of luck, is it?" By now Boysenberry's unyielding cordiality had grown positively macabre. "A lot of good can be done, you know, by a word in the right place." And with this insinuation the effort of tactfully shooting his bolt became too much for him, and from sheer nervousness his voice rose to a kind of shout.

"Oh, I see," said Fen, at last enlightened. "But I scarcely think that *my* recommendation—"

With a creditable effort Boysenberry regained control of his nerves. "You underestimate yourself, Professor Fen," he said; and when Fen, to whom this accusation was unfamiliar, vaguely demurred: "Ah, but indeed you do," Boysenberry reiterated firmly. "You must not, of course, imagine that I'm in any way *canvassing*. Dear me, no. But I thought that if you were to come across any of the members of the selection panel, socially as it were, and if you were just to mention that I was at least—ha, ha!—presentable..." And he left the sentence in mid-air, straightening his pince-nez and smoothing his hair in an attempt to make this suggestion colourable.

As an Open Sesame to the minutiae of Elphinstone's lunacy this could hardly be bettered, and Fen accepted it with a singular lack of scruple. "I know all the members of the selection panel intimately," he said, "and they are, on the whole, very suggestible. I think that perhaps I may be able to do something for you. These things are mostly arranged behind the scenes, you know." And in uttering this intolerable slander, Fen closed one eye in a knowing wink.

Enchanted, Boysenberry winked back. "I'm extremely obliged to you," he said. "Extremely obliged. And now—"

"And now, Elphinstone."

"Yes, yes, of course. Elphinstone." In his anxiety to be helpful Boysenberry rose agitatedly from his chair and then sat down again. "So long as I thought you a journalist...That is to say that in your case..." He picked up a sheet of paper and stared at it for a moment uncomprehendingly. "Elphinstone, yes. Naturally I shall be most happy to give you any information you require. Most happy...And I remember now that you have been engaged in a number of cases of a criminal nature. Perhaps, with regards to this dreadful affair last night..."

"Yes," said Fen. "It's that which interests me. The police, as you probably know, have formed the opinion that it was Elphinstone who committed the murder."

"So I understand." Boysenberry's elation rather abruptly evaporated at the reminder. "And no doubt," he added gloomily, "I shall be held responsible, inasmuch as it was from here that he escaped."

"If it's any consolation to you," said Fen, "I don't myself believe that he did it. That's why I'm here. And I expect it would help you if it could be proved that he did *not* do it."

"It would indeed," said Boysenberry eagerly. "I won't attempt to disguise from you the fact that if Elphinstone *is* proved to have killed this man, the consequences for me will be—ah—somewhat awkward. It will be said by ill-natured persons that I did not keep him under adequate restraint. Do you think, now"—he peered at Fen anxiously—"that such a—such a misfortune, let us say—would prejudice my chances of being appointed a Professor at Oxford?"

"I'm very much afraid that it would."

"Oh, dear," said Boysenberry in blank dismay. "Oh, dear... Well, we can only hope that the facts are not as they at present appear."

"And it may be feasible to demonstrate that they aren't." Wearying of these lengthy preliminaries, Fen spoke rather brusquely. "From what you know of his condition, would you say that Elphinstone was capable of killing?"

Boysenberry wriggled uncomfortably. "The difficulty is," he said, "that from first-hand observation I know very little of him. He had been here not much more than a week when he escaped—and in any case, it was quite a mistake that he was ever sent here at all."

"A mistake?"

"An error of card-indexing, I believe. This Home is not intended for complex cases such as his, but for the mild and intermittent forms of lunacy, and for patients who are convalescing and well on the way to recovery. By rights Elphinstone should have been sent to Climball or to Ferris Haugh. But someone blundered, as Browning so aptly puts it, and he was delivered here. And I don't know if you've noticed, but the Civil Service is a body whose mistakes are made so thoroughly and definitively that they can only be rectified by a procedure equally searching and elaborate...The moment Elphinstone and his file arrived I realised, of course, that he had been misdirected. But could I take immediate action to remedy this state of affairs? I could not—unless you are prepared to call the filling-in of forms 'action.' And the consequence was that he escaped, since we had not the proper means of restraining him."

"Most unfortunate," Fen agreed. "And I can understand, in that case, why you're unable to give an opinion about whether he might turn homicidal or not."

"Well, I wouldn't go quite so far as that," said Boysenberry hastily. "If I were pressed for a diagnosis, I should, I think, say that he was not homicidal; if I were *pressed*, that is," he reiterated, thereby nullifying whatever value his pronouncement might have had.

"Well, you may take it," said Fen, "that I am pressing you."

"Yes...On the other hand, it would be fatal to be too definite. The public is right in supposing madmen to be logical—and in that sense their actions can to some extent be foreseen...The only trouble is that the results of logic depend on its premises, and since lunatics are capable of changing their premises every two seconds, they can remain logical and yet still be totally unpredictable. For example..."

But Fen felt no desire for an example. "Yes, yes, I see all that," he interrupted. "And it leaves us exactly where we were to start with. Now, may I please hear what you know about Elphinstone's case history?"

"Certainly. Certainly you may." Boysenberry crossed with alacrity to the filing-cabinet and produced from it a pink file, which he laid open on the desk in front of him. "All the relevant papers are here, I think…Yes. Quite so…Well, in the first place, he's the son of normal middle-class parents; no previous madness in the family, so far as we've been able to discover. And his childhood and adolescence were perfectly normal, except that he developed, at about six years of age, a fixation about gloves."

"Ah," said Fen. Psychologists were unfortunate, he reflected, in that among technical jargons theirs alone had been so completely vulgarised as to have lost all impressiveness. Doctors could still awe their hearers with talk of oedema and ecchymosis, physicists with talk of dielectric constants, isotopes and photonic mass, chemists with talk of allotropic modification and multiple equivalence; it was only the luckless psychologist who lacked professional runes, for *trauma*, *complex*, *fixation* and the like had long since been deprived by popular usage of all hierophantic mystery…"A fixation," Fen repeated encouragingly.

"And the significance of it is not, I'm afraid, at all clear," Boysenberry went on. "In the normal way, a glove, being *hollow*, would of course be identified with the *womb*." He eyed Fen dubiously, as though scarcely expecting him to credit so grotesque an assertion. "But even if we make such an identification in this case, we are not," he admitted with candour, "very much helped by it. You must understand that in spite of having made great strides, our science is still not able to perceive and comprehend *every* quirk of the human mind."

Fen, who held the reactionary view that this prerogative was unlikely ever to be wrested from the Omnipotence, contrived none the less to look suitably sympathetic. "Just so," he murmured deferentially. "However, in Elphinstone's case it's the symptoms I need to know rather than the diagnosis."

"Ah." Boysenberry was perceptibly relieved. "To proceed, then...The glove-fixation was not accompanied by any other abnormality, and so, not unnaturally, the parents did nothing about it. And all was well until Elphinstone went to the University. There he undertook the study of philosophy, politics and economics—and our records show," said Boysenberry ingenuously, "that an interest in these subjects often leads on to total madness...However, that's by the way. The first noticeable sign that Elphinstone's mind was actually diseased lay in his growing conviction that President Woodrow Wilson was the most profound political thinker of our own or any age, an opinion which I'm told would be generally regarded as somewhat—ah—eccentric. At all events, his insistence on it resulted in his failing in his final examination...A year passes," said Boysenberry, relapsing dramatically into the historic present, "and when we next see him—the war being over—he is visiting Paris. And during this visit we get, for the first time, evidence that Elphinstone conceives himself to *be* Wilson, since he is found by an attendant in the Conference Room at Versailles making a long speech about—" here Boysenberry consulted the papers in front of him—"about the future of the Ruhr. On the attendant's remonstrating with him he seems to have reverted for a short period to comparative normalcy, but during the voyage back to England complete lunacy at last engulfed him. By some stratagem which remains obscure he assembled several young women on the boat-deck and, after, some preliminary remarks on the topic of international justice, ordered them to throw themselves instantly into the sea. They demurred at this—whereupon he seized two of them and threw them into the sea himself...I'm glad to say that the women were picked up not greatly the worse for their experience—but poor Elphinstone has from that time to this been uninterruptedly insane."

"Dear me," said Fen. "But wouldn't you say that his behaviour with these women indicated homicidal tendencies?"

"Well, no, not really. You must understand that he ordered the women to immolate themselves precisely because they *were* women and not men. A kind of *suttee* was what Elphinstone had in mind; and it was only when the women failed to cooperate that he took direct action. So although in certain circumstances he might just conceivably kill a female, I very much doubt if he would ever kill a man."

By now, however, Fen felt convinced that Elphinstone was capable of doing absolutely anything, and he was consequently not much impressed by this homiletic; as an argument against Elphinstone's having killed Bussy it was in any case hopelessly ineffectual—as also, indeed, was everything else that Boysenberry had told him so far. He cast about in his mind for some new line of approach. "The nudity," he said. "What about that?"

"Normal exhibitionism."

"And I gather that that is never simultaneous with the glove-fixation."

"No, never. If one interprets the glove-fixation as a womb-fixation, then by rights, of course, the two things *ought* to be simultaneous. But in fact—" and Boysenberry's tone betrayed some resentment at Elphinstone's failure to conform with the more elementary tenets of psychological science—"in fact, they are not."

"Are there any particular phobias?"

Boysenberry hesitated momentarily, and then said: "None—except, that is, things which are associated with his belief that he is Wilson."

"Such as?"

"Well, such as Clemenceau, for instance."

Clemenceau, Fen thought gloomily: there was not much illumination in that. Moreover, the interview was beginning to pall. If any proof existed that X, and not Elphinstone, had killed Bussy, then it was not likely to be found here. "I think—" he began—and was interrupted by a knock on the door. With a hasty word of apology Boysenberry bawled a permission to enter across the acres separating him from it. An attendant came in, accompanying an elderly male patient. They padded over to the desk.

"Firkin, sir," said the attendant. "You asked to see him before lunch."

"Oh, yes, so I did." Boysenberry was evidently displeased at the interruption; still, it might perhaps provide an opportunity for displaying his grasp of abnormal psychology to Fen. "Well," he said to the lunatic, "and how are we this morning?"

"None the better for seeing you," the lunatic answered.

Boysenberry assumed an expression of incisive scientific curiosity. "Now, why should you say that, I wonder?"

"I say it because you have such an ugly mug."

"Dear me." Boysenberry laughed uneasily. "Well, I've never prided myself on being handsome, exactly, but still, I should hardly—ha ha!—go so far as that."

"I," said the lunatic, amiably but with emphasis, "should go a hell of a sight further."

"Yes, well, Baines, I think you'd better take him away now and give him his meal." And when attendant and lunatic had peaceably departed: "Firkin is recovering fast," Boysenberry confided to Fen. "His is an interesting case, and in some respects similar to Elphinstone's. For instance, Firkin has a phobia about water, just as Elphinstone has a phobia about—" And here, belatedly realising what he was saying, Boysenberry checked himself and stared at Fen with dismay.

"Just," Fen echoed with deliberation, "as Elphinstone has a phobia about *what*?"

"About Clemenceau," Boysenberry stammered feebly. "About Clemenceau, I was going to say."

"Rubbish." Fen spoke with considerable severity. "You were going to say something quite different. Out with it. This evasiveness wouldn't be much appreciated in Oxford, you know."

"Oh, God."

"*What* is it that Elphinstone has a phobia about?"

Boysenberry's feeble essay in deceit collapsed like a pricked bladder. "I didn't tell the police when he escaped," he moaned, "and I haven't dared mention it since, for fear they'd be angry with me for not mentioning it in the first place."

"*What* is it that El—"

"But I had good reason for not mentioning it." Boysenberry was now sitting bolt upright and sweating with despair. "After all, it was my duty to make sure that Elphinstone wasn't frightened out of his senses—even further out of his senses, that's to say—by panic-stricken housewives waving lighted matches at him."

"*Lighted matches?*"

"There's one feature of his lunacy which has been quite invariable." In the extremity of his consternation Boysenberry now wholly collapsed, shrivelling up in his chair. "He is utterly unable to tolerate—by which I mean—"

"Utterly unable to tolerate *what*?"

"Fire," said Boysenberry weakly. "Fire."

❀ ❀ ❀

Three minutes later Fen was striding rapidly away from the Hall; a faint music which pursued him indicated that Boysenberry was seeking balm for his shaken nerves in "She is far from the Land"—but there would be needed a good deal more than that, Fen thought, if his self-assurance were to be wholly restored…It was a fairly long walk from the Hall to the Inn, and the Church clock was striking half past midday by the time he arrived there. His car—returned at some immoral hour of the night by Olive and Harry—stood in the yard, its front wing much dented by an impact with some immovable object. Near it, the non-doing pig was consuming a large Swede turnip, while Myra stood watching it.

"Still eating his head off," she commented with vague wonder. "Thank God, Farmer Lumley's coming to take him away again tomorrow. And there's another funny thing about him: he sometimes makes a barking noise, more like a dog."

"He looks to me," said Fen, climbing into the car, "like almost anything but a pig." He had started the engine when a line of enquiry occurred to him. "Myra," he said, "what do you know about the lunatic?"

"*Know* about him, my dear?"

"About the form his lunacy takes."

"Well, he thinks he's some American President, doesn't he? And they say he's got a passion for gloves."

"Do you think most people would know that?"

"Everybody knows it, my dear. The men as have been searching for him have talked a lot about him."

And that meant, Fen reflected as he drove in to Sanford Morvel, that anyone could have obtained the data necessary for counterfeiting the lunatic's presence in the golf-course shelter and his raid on Mr Judd's house: *Down with Taft* had obviously been a deliberate manoeuvre to associate Elphinstone with the theft of the knife. And for all that he had left Boysenberry weltering in the horrible conviction of his own insufficiency, Fen felt that there was reason to be grateful to the man; but for his occlusion of the vital fact, the death of Bussy would certainly have been attributed to Elphinstone—whose subsequent denials, even if he could have been brought to understand the accusation, would not have been believed; and X would once again have escaped the judgment and the rope...

Sanford Morvel police station was situated in the outskirts of the town, and consisted, as so many country police stations do, of two semi-detached brick houses knocked together into one. As Fen drove up, Wolfe and Humbleby were emerging from its gate, apparently on their way to lunch.

"Morning," said Wolfe cheerfully. "Thanks for sending us the village wooing last night. Its evidence'll be useful."

"One felt," said Humbleby, "that one's anxiety about the birth-rate had been premature."

"One's conclusions about Bussy have been premature," Fen answered, a shade grimly. "I've got some more evidence for you."

Wolfe's brow darkened with anxiety. "Let's hear it," he said quietly.

And Fen told them of his visit to Boysenberry. There was a long and very thoughtful silence when he had finished speaking.

"Well, we can't ignore that," said Humbleby eventually. "*Item*, there was only one person at the hut apart from Bussy and yourself. *Item*, that person was not Elphinstone, since a fire was lit, and Elphinstone can't tolerate fire."

"I'm still a bit doubtful," said Wolfe slowly, "about whether we're safe in accepting the evidence of these damned psychologists. They're capable of saying two things which are quite contradictory in the same breath."

"Agreed," Fen nodded. "And for most of Boysenberry's views I wouldn't give a brass farthing. But on this one point he's quite definite, and I wasn't able to shake him at all."

"We can't ignore it," Humbleby repeated with sudden authority. "The inquest this afternoon will have to be adjourned after identification. The case is open again...And where, I wonder, do we go from here?"

CHAPTER FOURTEEN

NURSE ROSALIND HICKEY took her eyes from her book and stiffened where she sat; a rising tide of abdominal discomfort engulfed her, and as it reached its zenith she closed her eyes and prayed devoutly for it to recede—which after the established way of its kind it presently did. The relief of its passing did not, however, provoke Nurse Hickey to any feeling of gratitude for the short-livedness of such pains; it provoked her, instead, to a ritual of commination against the bodily upsets which so infallibly ensued from a sudden transference to night duty. And indigestion was particularly humiliating. Though hardened by her vocation to the diverse and appalling feebleness of the human body, Nurse Hickey had never been able to feel resigned about indigestion. Had she been older, or even less personable, she might have endured it with philosophic equanimity; but being young and (her glass assured her) reasonably appealing, she found this particular affliction incongruous and shameful. She blushed—and this in spite of the fact that to all intents and purposes she was alone in the room.

Like all hospital rooms it smelt pervasively of ether and of surgical spirit. Above the iron bedstead hung a temperature chart, the violent fluctuations of whose graph might well have horrified even an uninstructed eye. On the locker stood a tray of medical impedimenta. Blanched chintz curtains stirred in a breeze from the open window, and the electric bulb over the bed had been shrouded in dark green cloth in order that no more than a minimum of light should filter through. Only where Nurse Hickey sat was there a pool of warmer light, from a small reading lamp on the dresser. It threw her shadow like a black crepe band across the bed, and she had only to lean forward an inch or two for the shadow to thicken and wholly submerge the motionless, bandaged girl who was her sole companion.

Nurse Hickey glanced at her watch. Ten past one. Nearly five hours to go...She got restlessly to her feet and went to the bed, where she stood looking down at the unconscious figure of her patient. Not bad-looking, Nurse Hickey conceded, and no doubt plenty of S.A. when she was in normal health. Not too well-off, though, to judge from her clothes. And one knew nothing at all about her, except that she was probably foreign. That would account for the fact that she had not had any visitors, whether friends or relations. On the other hand, her *name* was English enough...Nurse Hickey, her indigestion continuing in abeyance, grew sentimental. Probably this girl had a boyfriend somewhere; with her looks it was unbelievable that she hadn't. And now he'd be asleep in his own bed, not knowing how near to death she'd been. Well, with any luck she'd regain consciousness soon, and be able, perhaps, to tell them who he was, and they'd be able to send for him...

A tear came unbidden to Nurse Hickey's eye. Her kindly Irish heart doted on young love. And now, moving away from the bed, her thoughts turned to her own Reggie—he, too, slumbering unaware in the town below. She went to the curtains and opened them, thereby disturbing some creature of the night close outside, which rustled convulsively and then was silent. A square of yellow light from the window spread itself down the sloping lawn of the hospital. A rattle of china was distantly heard—Sister Bates, no doubt, trying to alleviate the tedium of her pernoctation by brewing tea.

Clouds partially obscured the moon, but it was possible to make out the low tower of Sanford Morvel Church, and the nearer roofs of the town; it was possible, by dint of belabouring the imagination, to fancy that one could make out that particular roof beneath which Reggie slept. At this very moment he might be dreaming of her, Rosalind; but more probably (she admitted to herself with considerable reluctance) he was not. What was certain was that he would be snoring, for Reggie, though handsome, vigorous and in every other way presentable, invariably snored. His adenoids, Nurse Hickey considered, ought to have been removed in early boyhood; and contemplating these offensive tumours, she frowned. They exemplified, to her, the besetting problem of life, the problem of how romance, which was real and beautiful, was to be reconciled with the body, also real but all too frequently unalluring. And for this melancholy dichotomy Nurse Hickey knew of no remedy. Love-making embodied it in the plainest and most indisputable fashion. A boy kissed you, and that was romantic. But then he went a bit further, and that, though it might be pleasant, was not *romantic*. And somehow the two aspects of love never quite fused, as of course they ought to...

In some such terms Nurse Hickey mused, as she stood gazing out of the window in the direction of the impervious Reggie. That Christianity offered a solution of her dichotomy she was wholly unaware. Like most of her generation, she was ignorant of even the elements of that hard and subtle doctrine. So she brooded, desponding, on indigestion and adenoids and sex and romantic love until such time as the first of these phenomena suddenly and without warning returned to plague her again.

Her face puckered with pain, she closed the curtains and stared wildly about the room in search of remedy. There was none. But in Matron's room, she remembered, bicarbonate of soda was to be found—and Matron was not in the hospital that night...Of course, she oughtn't to leave her patient, even for a minute, and the sensible course to take would be to ring for Nurse Temperley or Nurse Hall. But with Nurse Temperley and Nurse Hall her relations at the moment were far from cordial, and in such a summons they would be certain to find fresh matter for complaint. Better, after all, to go herself: her patient was no longer in danger, and no possible harm could come to her during so brief an absence...

Spurred on by a fresh spasm of anguish, Nurse Hickey fled from the room.

She reached Matron's Room without being observed, purloined a sufficient quantity of bicarbonate of soda, and returned with equal impunity. And the mere possession of that healing powder seemed to do her good, for the pains abated on this way back, and by the time her hand was on the doorknob were almost gone. She sighed with relief and opened the door.

And as she did so, fear struck at her like a knife.

The lights were out. The curtains were open again. Someone was bending over the girl on the bed. Starlight shone faint on the glass and metal of a hypodermic syringe.

For an instant Nurse Hickey stood numb with shock. Then her courage reasserted itself, her fingers sought and found the book on the dresser, and she flung it with vehemence and accuracy.

The hypodermic spun away like a dart, its delicate needle snapping in two against the wall. Momentarily, the person who held it hesitated, but the instinct of flight and safety prevailed. Clutching at slippery cloth in an attempt to arrest the almost headlong plunge through the window, Nurse Hickey was kicked in the face and hurled back onto the floor. She sprawled there, dazed, as the running footsteps receded down the lawn. Then she struggled to her feet and turned on the light over the bed.

The patient lay quiet and motionless, as before, but with her left arm bared and lying outside the covers. Sick with apprehension, Nurse Hickey groped for the fallen hypodermic and examined it with unsteady eyes.

It was full; it had not yet been used.

Nurse Hickey smiled a little, rang the bell and fainted.

❈ ❈ ❈

At nine-thirty on the following morning Wolfe telephoned to Fen at the Fish Inn and summarised for his benefit the events of the night.

"Jane Persimmons?" Fen echoed in bewilderment. "But why, in God's name, should anyone be trying to kill *her*?"

"The devil only knows." Wolfe's voice was the voice of a man who has slept too little and pondered too much. "This damned affair develops new ramifications every two seconds. Of course, the attack on the girl *may* not have anything to do with Bussy and Mrs Lambert. She's an oddly anonymous creature, and there's obviously some mystery about her, so the attack on her may be just coincidental with the other business. At the same time—"

"At the same time, one's instinct rebels against such coincidences." Fen nodded approval at the instrument. "Look here; can you let me have the details? I'm aware I've no conceivable right to meddle in all this, but still, I propose to do so as long as I'm allowed."

"My dear fellow, we shall be only too glad of your help. You've had experience of police work, and can't be considered an amateur. I'm in a mental fog; so also—as far as I can gather—is Humbleby. I can assure you, we shan't indulge in displays of professional jealousy if you can succeed in leading us out of it…I say, are you electioneering this morning?"

"Not seriously or long, I hope. Watkyn's probably got some tedious job mapped out for me, but I'm not due to meet him till half past ten."

"Well, come up to the hospital. Humbleby and I are going there now, to see if daylight supplies any kind of a clue. Of course, I was on the spot soon after the thing happened, but there was very little I could do or discover."

"You've got the girl guarded, I suppose?"

"Lord, yes." Wolfe laughed, but without humour. "My professional nerve is shaken, but not so seriously as to omit that. There's to be a tough policewoman in the room with her day and night, and I've instituted a system of triple checking on all drugs and injections that are administered to her, so as to be sure they haven't been tampered with. The hospital people don't like it much, but to hell with them."

"To hell with them indeed," Fen mildly concurred. "I'll drive over straight away, then." He rang off.

The Sanford Morvel hospital was a sturdy red brick building set in small but pleasant grounds, in no way dissimilar from a multitude of other such cottage hospitals scattered throughout the country. Wolfe and Humbleby were discovered on a garden seat, conversing despondently. They moved up to make room for Fen.

"Nothing useful so far." Red-eyed and yawning, Wolfe anticipated the inevitable question. "We haven't even been able to identify the stuff in the hypodermic. From all the doctors are able to tell us, it might be nothing more deadly than water. It *looks* like water, to me. And since luckily it was never administered, there are no physiological effects to go by."

"But presumably," said Fen, "it can be tested."

"We shall try," Humbleby answered. "But the analyst people aren't going to be pleased at having no guide whatever. There are about five thousand different tests for toxins. They'll use up what we give them in doing the first thousand or so, and if they haven't got a positive reaction by then, there'll be nothing more we can do about it."

"Rabbits," said Fen. "Dogs, toads."

Humbleby sighed. "Oh, yes. A licensed vivisection laboratory is the only hope. But even so, you know, it will probably take weeks."

"And the syringe?"

"Five c.c.," said Wolfe. "An unusually large one, I understand. It *may* ultimately be traced, but there's nothing to stop anyone buying a hypodermic anywhere at any time, so frankly I'm not hopeful. Still, we've ascertained that it doesn't belong to the hospital, which I suppose is progress of a kind."

"I take it you've also ascertained that no drugs are missing from the hospital stores?"

"I only wish we could. But bless their hearts, they can't tell me. There's apparently no check on quantities. They just go on using things until they run out, and then get some more. No locks have been tampered with—and that's absolutely all one can say on the subject."

"And it would be inane, no doubt, to ask if there were any fingerprints."

"It would, I'm afraid. Gloves are indicated. Nor are there any footmarks; the ground's far too hard. Nor are there any fragments of clothing. Clothing very seldom catches on things, if you come to think of it."

"What about the nurse? Can't she help?"

"A nice girl," said Humbleby thoughtfully. "And courageous. But no, she can't help. Assailant unidentifiable, a mere silhouette. Sex of assailant probably male, but there's no swearing to that. Size of assailant—too confused and alarmed to be certain. We're operating—or rather, *not* operating—in a factual vacuum...Well, well, it's common enough. There have to be clues in detective novels, but in actuality there are fewer than is generally supposed, and on occasion—as now none at all." Humbleby peered about him. "Or after all, *is* there to be a clue? Your sergeant, Wolfe, looks as if he might have found one."

They followed the direction of his gaze. An eager-looking young man in uniform hurried up to them with something lying on a handkerchief in the palm of his hand.

"Found it under a bush near the girl's window, sir," he reported.

"Good for you, Jimmy," said Wolfe.

They all examined the object—a small glass container, empty, and bearing the label of a well-known chemist. When they had looked their fill, Wolfe said: "Try it for prints, Jimmy."

The sergeant saluted and made off. "Insulin," Humbleby commented without evident comprehension. "I can't say I know much about that. They give it for diabetes, don't they?"

"So I believe." Wolfe nodded. "Of course, we can't be sure that that container has anything to do with the attack on the girl. In a hospital it's natural that—"

"Oh, come," Fen interrupted. "It's clear enough, I think. The effect of an overdose of insulin is to produce a hypo-glycaemic coma—just such a coma, to all outward appearance, as would probably precede death in a case of serious head injury." He sat upright with something like animation. "My God, what a damnably clever scheme! The girl will have been having injections, so the prick in her arm wouldn't arouse comment. And death would look like a perfectly natural conse-quence of the accident. There probably wouldn't even be an inquest. And if there *were* an inquest, there probably wouldn't be a post mortem. And if there *were* a post mortem, it certainly wouldn't occur to them to test the blood-sugar content. The thing is fool-proof. There isn't a doctor in the land who would have hesitated to write out the death certificate."

"Good God." Humbleby was shocked. "And am I to understand that this insulin can be obtained by anyone?"

"Certainly you are. There's no need to sign a poisons book, or even to have a doctor's prescription."

"And the quantity required?"

Fen frowned slightly. "Let's see; that was a five c.c. container, at forty units to the c.c. Two hundred units. It would probably be enough to kill, but I dare say he had more of the stuff on him, and was proposing to give a second injection and make sure of it...*Hell!*" Fen suddenly exclaimed. "He may have actually *given* one injection before the nurse got back. Wait for me." He got up and fled into the hospital.

Ten minutes later he reappeared, in a more tranquil state of mind. "All's well," he said. "No sign of trouble. In fact, it seems that the girl's rallying fast. They're expecting her to be conscious at any time now...And there's a point there, by the way. As I understand it, they didn't at first imagine she'd live."

"That's so," said Wolfe. "She took a turn for the better early yesterday morning—thereby, one presumes, provoking the attack last night."

"But how many people would *know* she was recovering?"

"Half the neighbourhood, I should think. These nurses gossip—who doesn't?—and it's got about that there's some kind of a mystery regarding this girl, so people are interested in her. No, I've considered that as a possible lead, and of course I'll do what I can about it, but I'm not sanguine."

Humbleby's eye was on Wolfe's ruddy complexion, and he seemed for a moment to contemplate some species of joke in connection with this last remark. But evidently he thought better of it, for he produced a packet of cheroots from his pocket, lit one, and after a pause for reflection merely said:

"Well, what now? To *me* it seems that our only course is to wait till the girl's fit to talk, and then see if we can't get some indication from her of a reason for the attack. It's not impossible that she knows something about Bussy's murder."

"Well, there's very little else we can do, except wait," said Wolfe with candour.

"You've made no progress, then," Fen enquired, "in the matter of Bussy?"

"None whatever. Material clues are lacking, inferences lead in and out of the same blind alley: how did X know that Bussy was going to turn up at the hut?" Wolfe stared at Fen with distrust. "Are you *sure* your conversation with Bussy couldn't have been overheard?"

"I'm positive of it. And I didn't tell anyone about it, and it's inconceivable to me that Bussy did."

Wolfe shrugged. "Then we're left with an impossibility." He hesitated, and then, apparently, came to a decision. "Look here, has it occurred to either of you that these cases may not, after all, be rationally related to one another?"

"It has certainly occurred to *me*," said Humbleby through a cloud of blue smoke. "You mean, I take it, that there's a homicidal maniac at work; that the connection between two of his victims—Bussy and Mrs Lambert—is fortuitous; and that we're wasting our time trying to establish a logical nexus for the three affairs, when the only thing they have in common is that one madman is responsible for all of them."

"That is what I mean," Wolfe agreed. "I wouldn't, of course, now identify this madman with Elphinstone."

"Nor even, necessarily, with the person who was blackmailing Mrs Lambert."

"Quite so."

Humbleby turned to Fen. "And you, Professor? What do you think?"

"I think you're talking nonsense. Homicidal maniacs don't contrive murder methods which simulate natural death. No, I stick to our original notion: that X blackmailed Mrs Lambert, killed her to prevent discovery, killed Bussy because Bussy was on his track, and attempted to kill this girl for a reason which we've yet to discover."

Humbleby sighed. "It's the better hypothesis, I admit. But for the one besetting problem, it fits the facts very much more snugly. Well, well, we shall see."

"And until the girl's fit to talk," said Wolfe, "there's one job we can get on with—I mean breaking open that box I took from her room at the Inn just after the accident. I feel I'm justified in doing that now."

"Ah," said Fen. "Let me know if it's anything interesting, won't you?" He made his farewells and departed.

CHAPTER FIFTEEN

IT IS NO part of my intention, in this brief though salutary narrative, to describe the progress of Fen's election campaign. And indeed, details are needless, since the intelligent reader can easily infer them from what has already been said. Shepherded by Captain Watkyn, Fen toured the constituency, was orotund in village halls and at street corners, disrupted with canvassing the matutinal labours of housewives, chatted affably and encouragingly with the small but gallant band of his active supporters, and in general piled *cliché* on *cliché* with an ingenuity worthy (as Captain Watkyn, with the air of one who has coined a new and striking turn of phrase, on one occasion remarked) of a better cause.

But disenchantment lay heavy on him, and be performed these functions conscientiously but without zeal. A repugnance for the whole transaction grew on him hourly, and upon the editing of Langland he looked back with a nostalgia which students of that malignant poet will scarcely be able to credit. His meetings, though numerically small, were almost always enthusiastic, and he might have derived some consolation from that. By a smooth and earnest utterance, in which no single sentence lacked platitude of form or content, he could undoubtedly hold and stir his hearers. But the pleasure to be had from this rapidly palled. An expert conjuror may initially be gratified if his audience supposes the tricks to be worked by real magic; if this attitude persists, however, he will soon grow peevish and discontented. And thus it was with Fen. He found himself in the position of an actor whose miming is so plausible that the emotions he presents come to be universally regarded as real and not artificial, and to whose skill, in consequence, no tribute is ever paid.

He was haunted, moreover, by a growing fear that he might actually be elected. This possibility had not, at the time of his arrival in Sanford Angelorum, seemed particularly daunting, but a few days of campaigning gave it a more ominous look. A whole-time preoccupation with democratic politics, he rapidly discovered, is not easily imposed on a humane and civilised mind. In no very long time the gorge rises and the stomach turns. And the prospect of five years spent drooping in and out of lobbies, crying "Oh!" from back benches, arguing in committee rooms, corresponding with crazy constituents and suffering without protest that which the House of Commons supposes to be wit—all this, conceivably stored up for him in what Captain Watkyn would have called the womb of time, Fen was beginning to find inexpressibly dispiriting. He had money of his own; he had been a Professor at Oxford for nearly ten years; he had felt that a change of occupation would be good for his soul. And he now saw with belated clarity that he had been mistaken. He might, of course, have withdrawn his candidature, and there were moments when he seriously considered doing this; but a certain native obstinacy, combined with a curiosity as to the ultimate issue, kept him in the field. And if the worst happened, the Chancellor could probably be induced to give him the Chiltern Hundreds...

Polling was fixed for the Saturday. By the Thursday, the state of the parties defied analysis. Labour expected a gain, but was far from being confident of victory. And the Conservatives would have been happy enough had it not been for Fen, whose programme, in so far as it was ascertainable at all, leaned rather to the Right than to the Left, and who was expected in consequence to seduce a certain number of Conservative voters from their proper allegiance: an expectation which was strengthened by Strode's comparative lack of personality.

"The fact is, old boy, it's anybody's guess," said Captain Watkyn, who was as yet unaware of Fen's waning enthusiasm. "And your own chances aren't half bad. Now, if we could only get that ruddy loudspeaker van working again…"

The loudspeaker van's first excursion had taken it from Sanford Morvel to Sanford Angelorum, and thence a short distance towards a minute village romantically and quite inappositely named Dawn. When about three miles from the nearest telephone it had, however, broken down simultaneously in all departments, and it was now back at the electrician's undergoing treatment appropriate to its relapse. Fen would have been delighted to have abandoned it altogether, but for Captain Watkyn the whole campaign was tending to resolve itself into a kind of duel between himself and the van, and he declined to hear of such a thing. In this matter, he gave Fen to understand, his professional reputation was at stake; by hook or by crook he was going to have the damned van back on the road by polling day; and Fen, after arguing the point feebly for some minutes, was forced to give in.

Even more disconcerting than the loudspeaker van was the problem of Mr Judd. Mr Judd had run politically amok. His early reluctance to be active in Fen's cause had given place with horrid swiftness to an excess of zeal which both Fen and Captain Watkyn found a serious embarrassment. He insisted on taking the chair at all meetings; he orated unquenchably;

he spent hours in Sanford Morvel Library assembling a factual indictment of the party system in politics and elaborating this into a philosophy of history. And upon such topics as the origins of Whiggery he talked at Fen and Captain Watkyn in season and out, to their consternation and dismay.

At first it seemed probable to Fen that all this constituted an attempt to please Jacqueline, but in view of the disinterested vehemence of Mr Judd's goings-on he was presently compelled to abandon the theory. Mr Judd, it became plain, was reacting as only a normally retiring man can react to the excitements of public life. They had gone to his head like (I quote Captain Watkyn again) strong wine, and whereas previously he had shunned them, now he could not have enough of them. Fen and Captain Watkyn found being in his company a severe trial of their patience, for Captain Watkyn had never had any interest in political problems as such, and Fen had temporarily lost whatever interest he might previously have felt. They contemplated Mr Judd's unforeseen fervour with the fatalistic horror of Frankenstein confronted for the first time with his monster. And Mr Judd plunged unheeding on, like the broom of the sorcerer's apprentice, and neither Fen nor Captain Watkyn could think of any spell powerful enough to stop him.

"Opsimath," said Fen dismally. "Having embarked on politics for the first time late in life, Judd had got obsessed with them; just as a child, on discovering it can write its own name, *goes on* writing its own name until it drops down from exhaustion."

"Ah," said Captain Watkyn sagely.

It is undeniable that Mr Judd's zeal won many supporters for Fen; but his efforts may have been nullified to some extent by the editor of *The Sanford Advertiser* and *Peek Gazette*, who, in his determination to requite the service rendered him by Fen's father, disastrously overstepped the bounds of good sense. He published, on the Thursday, an issue which overtly

flouted those great canons of impartiality in British journalism
to which British journalists are so assiduous in calling our
attention, by extolling Fen and his candidature to the virtual
exclusion of all else. Even Captain Watkyn, whose optimism
constituted a necessary adjunct of his livelihood and so was not
easily quenched, felt some misgivings.

"The fact is, old boy, it looks deuced fishy," he said. "It
looks like what it is, a put-up job, and I'm afraid it'll do you
more harm than good. Astonishing how tactless some of these
journalist johnnies are."

By this time, of course, there were at large in the neighbourhood journalist johnnies of a more portentous kind than
the editor of *The Sanford Advertiser* and *Peek Gazette*. As
has already been said, the Sanford election, in its beginnings,
received scant attention from the nation at large; a few of the
more popular newspapers came out with small heads like
"Don-Detective Enters Politics," but the pressure on their
space was too overwhelming to allow of more than the briefest
paragraphs. The outbreak of murder, however, and the escape
of Elphinstone, offered more promising material, and moreover, by some unfathomable logic, enhanced the interest of the
election; and soon political and crime reporters were rubbing
shoulders in the Sanford bars and, in the intervals of quarrelling fiercely about their accommodation, foraging abroad for
pabulum for the presses. Since Fen was involved both in the
politics and in the crime, he was a good deal sought after. But
his Machiavellian attempts to barter inside information about
the murders for political support produced a deadlock. No
journalist on the spot—as he might have known, and probably did—was in a position to make such bargains, and this
was just as well, since Fen did not possess any inside information about the murders and, if his offers had been accepted,
would have had no recourse but to invent some: an exercise in
which, though undoubtedly skilled at it, he would ultimately

have been detected. The reporters were consequently obliged to content themselves with Mr Judd, who was prepared to talk inexhaustibly about both crime and politics. His *obiter dicta*, on the former subject at any rate, were widely published; Annette de la Tour's sales rose perceptibly, and Annette de la Tour's publisher took to drinking Laffitte instead of Margaux with his lunch. A very general contentment prevailed.

❀ ❀ ❀

On leaving Wolfe and Humbleby at the hospital, Fen went to the White Lion to seek out Captain Watkyn. He was discovered lurking unhappily in the lounge under the compelling, ancient-mariner-like eye of Mr Judd, whose political albatross, the party system, had acquired additional plumage from the previous afternoon's work in the public library, and who was now expounding this at length. Fen silenced him for sufficiently long to ascertain that no arrangement had been made for that morning, and then uncivilly fled, driving back under a cloudless sky to the Fish Inn.

He procured coffee, and drank it perched on the garden roller, brooding disjointedly over the election and the crimes. Within the Inn, Mr Beaver and his coadjutors hammered monotonously away, presently introducing a variation in the form of a saw whose voice was the voice of a corn-crake in intolerable agony. Fen rose hurriedly and left the precincts. He subscribed wholeheartedly to the view of Sir Max Beerbohm that nothing so effectively inhibits thought as Going for a Walk, but at the moment no better alternative offered itself. He set off rather dejectedly along the village street.

There was one turning which he had not so far investigated—a lane which led up past the Rectory and which terminated, according to an ancient signpost, at the town of Wythendale, twelve miles away. He accordingly set off along it, and presently paused at the Rectory gate to survey both the incumbent's dwelling—a large, nondescript grey building—and the incumbent himself, who, clad in disreputable flannels, was bending down to peer at a diseased-looking hollyhock in the front garden. From these objects Fen's attention soon strayed to a brightly hued insect which was perched on a twig beside the gate, and he prodded it experimentally with his forefinger. It at once stung him viciously and flew away. Fen, who lacks stoicism, uttered a cry of anguish and dismay, at which the Rector abruptly straightened up to stare in his direction. And in the instant following, a small white coffee-cup was projected from one of the upper windows of the Rectory and sailed past within a centimetre of the Rector's nose.

CHAPTER SIXTEEN

Now EVEN IN the most trivial afflictions Fen regards
it as the inalienable duty of his fellow-men to offer him instant
sympathy and relief, and to continue offering them during all
the lengthy period of his complainings. He would not, therefore, normally have considered it other than entirely right and
seemly that the Rector, at his cry, should hasten towards him
with every appearance of the deepest anxiety and solicitude;
where the pastoral duties of the clergy are concerned, Fen is
a particularly exigent and fussy sheep. The present circumstances, however, gave him pause. It was no doubt the Rector's
business, after the first shock of surprise at being assailed with
a coffee-cup, to thrust his own problem into the background of
his mind and rush to succour Fen; but it was a little surprising
that he should so completely ignore the coffee-cup as not even
to glance in the direction whence it had come. It now lay,
unbroken, on a flower-bed near him; he could not conceivably
have failed to see it, or at least to feel the wind of its passing;
yet he might, to judge by his total failure to react in any of the

expected ways, have been entirely unconscious of it. By the time he arrived at the Rectory gate, Fen was regarding him with some distrust. Moreover, it quickly appeared that the Rector's anxiety was functioning in the wrong direction.

"What did you see?" he demanded. "What was it you saw?"

"Saw?" Fen frowned reprovingly. "I saw a coffee-cup thrown at you, if that's what you mean."

"But your cry anticipated the throwing of the cup, if I'm not much mistaken. Can it be that you saw the thrower?"

"No, it can't," said Fen uncivilly. "I uttered an involuntary exclamation because I'd just been stung, and that most painfully. Look." He held out his forefinger for inspection.

"Stung. Ah." The Rector's anxiety grew visibly less urgent, and he put on a pair of horn-rimmed spectacles in order to examine the injured part. "Dear me, yes. By a bee, by a wasp?"

"By, I think, some venomous tropical insect."

"Blue bag," said the Rector. "It must be treated with blue bag." He paused, and his face assumed a rather artificial expression of great shrewdness. "But there is, I am afraid, one thing which I am bound to ask before inviting you inside. Are you by any chance connected with the Psychical Research Society?"

"The Psychical Research Society?" Fen echoed in surprise. "No, indeed I'm not."

"And you would hardly—ha! ha!—be a believer in the supernatural."

"Well, I wouldn't go so far as to say that," Fen answered rather impatiently—and at once saw that he had said the wrong thing, for the Rector's expression changed, at the reply, from shrewdness to definite apprehension. "However," Fen added hurriedly, "I'm prepared, if you wish it, to suspend my belief for as long as it takes to be treated with blue bag."

The Rector appeared to ponder deeply; and eventually

arriving at a decision: "Come in, then," he said, unlatching the gate. "I'm afraid you'll be thinking me very discourteous and unready to help, but the fact is that what has just occurred puts me in a rather serious quandary."

"The sting?" said Fen, whose sufferings continued to hold precedence, in his own mind, over all else.

The Rector was leading the way along the path and round the side of the Rectory. "No, no," he said over his shoulder. "The coffee-cup." And by a tulip tree he halted with such abruptness that Fen nearly cannoned into him. "It would be useless, no doubt, to imagine that you are not curious."

Fen's thoughts were preoccupied with blue bag, so it was rather perfunctorily that he agreed that such a supposition would, indeed, be false.

"Exactly so. And I feel that I must therefore take you into my confidence...I am right, of course, in thinking that you are Professor Fen?"

"Perfectly right."

"My name is Mills." And apparently feeling that this intelligence would be sufficient to occupy Fen's mind for the time being, the Rector resumed his progress, fetching up shortly at the back door. Fen followed him in a dazed condition.

"Mrs Flitch," the Rector called, opening the back door. *"Mrs Flitch."*

A small, intense, untidy-looking elderly woman appeared, clutching a mop. "Yes, sir," she said breathlessly. "Yes, sir, yes, sir."

"Blue bag, Mrs Flitch. This gentleman has been stung."

"There now," said Mrs Flitch, "Well I never." She retired, exclaiming continuously, into the kitchen, and was heard opening drawers and cupboards. Presently she returned with the blue bag, and Fen dabbed it on the sting. It did not seem to do much good. He gave it back to Mrs Flitch and the Rector, whose thoughts during these proceedings had transparently been elsewhere, took him by the arm and led him to a wooden seat on the lawn behind the Rectory.

"And now, to resume what I was saying," said the Rector. "About the coffee-cup, that is."

The pain, Fen thought, was abating slightly; presumably blue bag took time to do its healing work. And he felt more capable, now, of attending to the matter of the coffee-cup, which, he began to realise, was decidedly queer. "Yes?" he said encouragingly.

"You will, I hope, keep what I am going to tell you a dead secret." The Rector briefly glowered at Fen, as though attempting to assess his capacity for reticence. "Indeed, I must ask you to promise that. There is nothing of an immoral or—um—criminal nature in what I have to say, but *serious inconvenience* may be caused if it leaks out."

"Ah," said Fen without comprehension. "Well, you may rely on my discretion. And please understand that you're under no obligation to tell me anything at all, if you don't wish to do so."

"But it will be better for me to do so, I think. And besides, it would be unfair to you not to do so." The Rector hesitated, drawing a deep breath. "You will have heard," he said, "of Borley Rectory."

"Most people have, I think. And there's no doubt, to my mind, that it was in some fashion haunted."

"It was very thoroughly investigated," the Rector remarked, "over a period of years."

"Quite so."

"In fact, the incumbent can have had very little peace."

"From the poltergeist."

"No. From the investigators."

"Well, now you mention it, I suppose they must have been a bit trying."

"Sealed doors," said the Rector. "Microphones. Vigils. Seismographs, for all I know."

"I scarcely think—"

"But you admit the general principle."

"What general principle?" Fen asked—vaguely, contemplating his finger.

"That the investigation," saw the Rector with patience, "must have constituted a great hindrance."

"Well, yes, but—"

"A fact which I anticipated many years ago."

"Indeed."

"You perceive my drift?"

"I'm afraid not," said Fen, shaking his head.

The Rector sighed. "The point is, you see, that I have a poltergeist—that there is a poltergeist *here*."

If he had offered to levitate, Fen could scarcely have been more dumbfounded.

"Do you mean to say," he exclaimed convulsively, "that that coffee-cup—"

"It was thrown by the poltergeist. Yes."

"But are you *sure* you have a poltergeist? A more natural explanation would be—"

"A more natural explanation, Professor Fen, is not possible."

"Perhaps your housekeeper—"

"No, no. The thing continues to polter even when she is quite certainly miles away."

"A practical joker, then."

"A practical joker whose operations continue uninterruptedly for eighteen years," said the Rector dryly, "is very much less credible, to me at any rate, than a supernatural explanation."

"*Eighteen years?*"

"I have been Rector here for eighteen years, and the start of the disturbances was coincident with my arrival."

Fen gazed at him aghast. "But have you done nothing about it?"

"Well, at first I was naturally very distressed, and considered applying to the Bishop for a licence for exorcism—as soon, that is, as I had ascertained that it was not some form of delusion or practical joke. But the plain fact is that in a week or two I got quite used to it."

"Remarkable," said Fen with restraint.

"The point is, you see, that whatever may be the case with other poltergeists, this particular one has never inspired in me, or for that matter of that in anyone else, the conventional feelings of terror. It is *materially* a nuisance, since it throws things about and they have to be picked up again and replaced; but the emotional effects normally associated with such—um—phantasms are completely lacking. So although the thing was undeniably tiresome, rather in the way that defective plumbing would be tiresome, I decided eventually that the publicity which would inevitably follow an attempt to get rid of it would be even *more* tiresome. Moreover, my poltergeist has intelligence of a sort, and I feared that if an investigation were set on foot it would refrain from its activities while the investigators were present and thus involve me in the suspicion of insanity. All things considered, it seemed better to leave it alone, and I've never yet regretted doing so."

Fen contemplated him for a moment in silence, seeking in his face for some evidence that this was an elaborate leg-pull. But he saw none. The Rector, though he might be deluded, was undeniably sincere. And other cases of poltergeist disturbances extending over a long period of years were, Fen reflected, tolerably well authenticated. Moreover, the Rector's reactions were understandable—except, of course, that he must suffer considerable financial loss from the poltergeist's depredations…This issue Fen ventured to raise.

"Well, no," said the Rector. "For some reason which I haven't fathomed, things the poltergeist handles never break. That coffee-cup is an instance—and I know that even if it had hit the wall it would have remained intact. There are many recorded instances of the same phenomenon in other hauntings of a like kind. And my poltergeist is also in the best traditions in that although it constantly hurls small objects at Mrs Flitch and myself, it has never yet succeeded in actually hitting either of us. In the first weeks I was naturally apprehensive that it might, but since it invariably failed to do so my anxiety soon wore off, and nowadays I pay no attention to such occurrences at all."

"And apart from throwing things," said Fen rather faintly, "what else does it do?"

"It pulls out drawers and drops them on the floor. That's sheer rowdyism, and really rather trying at times. It also *raps*—on walls apparently, but it's difficult to tell. Oh, and it occasionally makes a stupid howling noise on the stairs, which I imagine is intended to frighten, but which is actually no more alarming than a bicycle bell. That's all, I think—there's no writing, and I've certainly never *seen an apparition* of any kind. When I first came here I used to bound about the house trying to catch sight of one, but it was quite useless, and I've long since ceased to trouble about it."

Fen produced a handkerchief and wiped the perspiration from his brow. "But in view of all this," he observed, "you must have found it very difficult to keep the matter secret."

"Well, not so difficult as you might suppose. The disturbances do not usually begin until about ten in the evening—daylight manifestations, such as you witnessed, have only occurred twice before, and then, fortunately, without being seen by outsiders."

"But your night's rest it must surely be very disturbed?"

The Rector frowned. "At first," he admitted, "it *was* very disturbed—but I soon succeeded in domesticating the thing."

"In *domesticating* it?"

"Well, in training it, if you prefer the word; much as one trains a cat to be clean or a dog to come to heel. The means were simple, though I only discovered them by accident. The creature was rapping away one night at one a.m. when I was trying to get to sleep after a very tiring day, and in exasperation I sat up in bed and rapped back at it, much more loudly. And it was so astonished that it immediately fell silent. Thereafter I always replied in kind whenever it created a pother at an unseemly hour, and it gradually came to realise that it must keep quiet after about twelve midnight. On the whole it's been very faithful to this arrangement…I considered, of course, the possibility of driving it away completely by the method I've spoken of, but to be quite candid, such a scheme seemed to me needlessly brutal. The thing clearly enjoyed its preposterous goings-on; they did no one any serious harm; and since I might conceivably worsen its condition by scaring it off, I felt it my duty as a Christian priest to let it alone."

Fen said: "Well, yes, I suppose that with a little luck you could hush the whole thing up. And I certainly don't blame you for doing so."

"It's meant that I've been unable to have people to stay with me, said the Rector, "and I'm afraid that on many occasions I must consequently have appeared most inhospitable. But on the whole, as I say, I've never regretted taking the course I have taken."

"And what about your housekeeper? What does she think of it all?"

For the first time during his recital the Rector looked uneasy; he stared, embarrassed, at his boots.

"That," he said, "is the one feature of the whole affair which lies really heavily on my conscience. Mrs Flitch has her own explanation of the matter, but unluckily it is far from being a true one; and although I did not suggest it to her in the first place and have never specifically concurred with it, I'm bound to say that I've always been too pusillanimous actually to deny it. And this is the more sinful of me in that her explanation reflects a great deal of quite undeserved credit on myself…It seems that in her younger and more impressionable days someone gave Mrs Flitch a translation of Anatole France's novel *Thaïs*, and that reading this had a very profound effect on her mind. Early on in the book there are descriptions of the various temptations undergone by the coenobite hermits in the desert outside Alexandria—and Mrs Flitch, confronted for the first time by the activities of the poltergeist, jumped to the erroneous conclusion that these had a similar—um—nature and purpose in relation to myself. It is her view that what she herself witnesses is only a part of the matter; that unseen by her"—a glint of humour came momentarily to the Rector's eye—"and on account of my extreme sanctity, spectral harpies foul me with their droppings as I sit writing at my desk, and alluring courtesans make nightly trial of my continence…In all this, I'm afraid, she greatly overestimates my importance in the eyes of the Devil, who no doubt has better uses for his courtesans than to assign them so regularly to me." He sighed deeply. "And I have been most guilty in not once and for all dispelling the illusion. Mrs Flitch, you see, is for some reason quite clear in her own mind that these—um—supposititious temptations must not be revealed to any outsider, and I have shamelessly taken advantage of her self-imposed reticence by failing to remove its cause. I shall not easily be forgiven—and particularly since my ultimate motive is nothing more elevated than a desire to pander to my own comfort by keeping the Psychical Research Society away."

With as much gravity as he could muster, Fen gave it as his opinion that the sin was venial. "And have you," he asked, "your own explanation of the phenomena?"

The Rector, who up to now had been almost uninterruptedly serious, chuckled suddenly.

"I sometimes suspect," he said, "that my poltergeist must be a demon who has been expelled from Hell for incurable incompetence…But no, I haven't really any explanation. At first I thought a good deal about the business, and read all the available literature on the subject. But I found that no one theory was any more provable or plausible than the next, so I soon gave up worrying about it, and haven't, indeed, done so for years. Custom, Professor Fen, is an unspeakable blessing. I'm so used to my poltergeist now that weeks on end pass without a recollection of it ever entering my head."

He paused, gazing absently at the upstairs windows of the Rectory, and then turned to Fen with a charming smile.

"Now be honest," he said. "Have you believed a word I've been saying?"

"Why not?" said Fen. "I think the evidence for the existence of poltergeists is virtually unassailable; I see nothing specially unlikely in there being one here; and I find your own reactions to it quite natural. Moreover, if you should happen to be pulling my leg, it's at least a quite amusing leg-pull, and hence not at all to be regretted."

The Rector chuckled again. "Fair enough, sir," he said. "And whether you think it's a leg-pull, or insanity, or hard fact, I shall still be grateful if you'll keep it to yourself."

"I'll certainly do that."

"And the finger—"

"Is much less painful, thank you." Fen glanced at his watch and stood up. "And now I think I ought to be getting back to lunch. Many thanks for the blue bag, and I'm sorry to have interrupted your gardening."

"My dear fellow, I've enjoyed our talk very much indeed, and it's been a great relief to be able to confide to someone my behaviour as regards Mrs Flitch...I'll walk with you to the gate. How is your campaign going?"

"As well, I think, as can be expected. I'm getting rather tired of it, to tell you the truth."

"Ah. Well, you've certainly come down here at an eventful time. That unhappy lunatic, who I gather is still at large...And then, these dreadful murders, and the wicked attempt last night on the poor girl at the hospital. I saw her about once or twice, and do you know, her face struck me as being in some indefinable way familiar."

"Really?" Fen was interested. "Did you think you'd come across her somewhere before?"

"No, not that exactly," said the Rector thoughtfully, "because I have a good memory for faces. My feeling was..."

But for the moment Fen was not destined to be apprised of what the Rector's feeling was. They rounded the side of the house as he spoke, and came to an open window on the ground floor. The Rector's glance, at first resting incuriously on it, grew suddenly fixed; and he halted.

"Bless my soul!" he ejaculated.

Fen could see no occasion for his surprise. The room into which they were looking was nothing more remarkable than an ordinary, rather gloomy clerical study, furnished with dark stuffs and mahogany. In view of what he had heard it was not impossible, however, that the Rector was seeing a ghost, and Fen peered attentively at the room's obscurity in the vague hope of being similarly favoured.

"What is it?" he demanded.

"The field-glasses," said the Rector. "Those field-glasses on the table beside the window. They've come back."

"Come back?"

"The other afternoon—let's see, it must have been Monday—I took them out with me on a walk, since I'm interested in bird-watching and for that they're naturally indispensable. In Porson's Wood I sat down for a moment to rest, laying them on the ground beside me, and when I proceeded on my way I very stupidly and absent-mindedly left them there. Not more than ten minutes can have—um—elapsed before I realised what had happened and returned to fetch them. But by that time they had been taken, and in view of the almost universal dishonesty which prevails nowadays I never thought to see them again. Well, well, this is very pleasing."

"But the way in which they've apparently been returned," said Fen, "is surely odd. If I find something belonging to someone else, and wish to return it, I normally knock at the door and hand it over...And by the way, how would anyone know they were yours?"

"My name is written in ink on the inside of the strap...But I agree with you"—the Rector was mildly perplexed—"that this method of replacement has certainly an element of the—um—surreptitious about it."

"Though of course that would not apply if the house had been empty at any time during the period in which the glasses were returned."

"They were not there when I went to bed last night," said the Rector. "I'm confident of that. And as it happens, neither Mrs Flitch nor myself has left the premises since then. Yes, it is undeniably strange—though I dare say that if one could only think of it there is some perfectly reasonable explanation."

A vague suspicion was burgeoning in Fen's mind. "Would you object," he said, "if I were to make an experiment with the glasses?"

"An experiment?"

"I want to see if there are any fingerprints on them."

"Dear me." The Rector was startled. "By all means do so, though I fail to see why—"

"It's no more than a shot in the dark. I wonder, now, if you could provide me with a soft-haired brush and some fine powder?"

"The brush I can certainly manage. And Mrs Flitch uses face powder, if that would do. Lipstick I know she considers ungodly, but as regards face powder her views are more—um—liberal...Mrs Flitch," the Rector called. "Mrs *Flitch*."

Mrs Flitch's head emerged from a window above them like a cuckoo from a cuckoo-clock. Informed of what they required, she retreated without perceptible surprise to obtain it. The Rector led Fen indoors and into the study, producing from a drawer in an over-full roll-top desk a small new paint-brush. And presently Mrs Flitch joined them with a box of peach-coloured face powder called *Nuits d'extase*.

"Now," said the Rector.

Fen plied the brush, spreading powder carefully over the field-glasses and blowing it off again. A haze of *Nuits d'extase* enveloped them.

"Well?" The Rector was leaning forward eagerly.

"There are," Fen answered, "no fingerprints on the glasses at all: which means that they've been thoroughly wiped."

The implications of this curious circumstance did not very rapidly penetrate the Rector's intelligence. "Amazing," he remarked—but less with real comprehension than in the voice of a man who has watched a dog do a difficult trick. "Amazing. No doubt the glasses got dirtied in some way, and were cleaned by the person who returned them."

Fen, to whom this notion had not occurred, was a little taken aback. But he recovered himself after a moment, saying: "Even if you clean a thing, you almost inevitably leave one or two prints on it. On these glasses there are *none*."

"But what," said the Rector blankly, "do you think is the significance of that?"

"I haven't," Fen replied with truth, "the smallest notion. But I'm bound to assume that someone who has been in possession of these glasses is very anxious that the fact shouldn't be known."

The Rector sneezed. "It's the powder," he apologised weakly. "Mrs Flitch. Mrs *Fl*—oh, you're here already. We shall need the use of a clothes-brush, Mrs Flitch, if we are not both to be suspected of embracing young women."

Mrs Flitch, not altogether displeased at this worldly utterance, fetched a clothes-brush and applied it to each of them in turn. "Dear me," said the Rector, sniffing like a hound at fault, "this is a very sensuous perfume, Mrs Flitch, and it makes me wonder what you get up to on your evenings off." It was clear from Mrs Flitch's expression, however, that she had had enough of worldly utterances for the moment, and the Rector, perceiving this, hurriedly changed the subject. "Well, now, Professor Fen, I can't pretend to compete with you in such affairs as this of the field-glasses...Do you suppose that they can have anything to do with all these other—um—dreadful occurrences we have been hearing of?"

"It is possible," said Fen guardedly, "though, at present I can't imagine what the connection is...And now I really must be going. You've been most forbearing and kind."

The Rector accompanied him down the path towards the gate. Showers of pebbles were flung at them from an upper window.

"Really, this is too much," the Rector muttered. "Excuse me, please."

He went back along the path and in at the front door, and was heard toiling upstairs. Shortly afterwards there came an angry rapping, and the showers of pebbles ceased. The Rector appeared at a window.

"That's stopped it," he said cheerfully. "Do call in any time you're passing, won't you? I've very much enjoyed our chat... Good morning to you." He vanished from sight.

(HAPTER SEVENTEEN

IT WAS WITH a mind occupied rather with field-glasses than with poltergeists that Fen made his way back to the Inn. Decisive enlightenment, he felt sure, lay somewhere just outside the perimeter of his thoughts; it hovered there, half glimpsed and unspeakably tantalising; but for the moment no amount of blandishment availed to bring it out into the open, and the effect of this was as exacerbating as a physical itch. Fortunately, his arrival at the Inn coincided with a scene sufficiently uncommon to put a temporary stop to his reflections.

Watched with proprietary interest by Myra, the non-doing pig was being taken away again. Two men had hold of it by the front and hind legs respectively, and were hoisting it with extreme difficulty onto a small van, while it screamed and struggled incessantly. The job was at last completed and the backboard of the van fastened; peering in consternation over it, like a malefactor being conveyed to a gaol, the non-doing pig was driven away. But now occurred a striking demonstration of animal fidelity. Before the van had rounded the bend in the village street, the non-doing pig had taken a running jump at the backboard, cleared it by a narrow margin, and landed heavily on its head in the road.

Consternation ensued. Both Fen and Myra screamed at the van to stop, and this it ultimately did. They all gathered about the non-doing pig where it lay in the dust. It was not dead, but clearly it was none the better for its experience.

After some rather valueless discussion as to the best course to pursue, it was again loaded onto the van, this time without resistance, and removed to a veterinary surgeon. The last Fen saw of it was a small and infinitely reproachful eye fixed upon Myra.

"Poor thing," said Myra compassionately. "I really believe he can't bear to leave me. I shouldn't have sold him, not if he'd been a bit more seductive, like. But he ate so much, that was the real trouble...There's been a phone message for you, my dear."

"Oh?"

"From the Superintendent. He says will you look in at the police station in Sanford Morvel some time when you have a moment."

"I think," said Fen, "that I'd better go over there straight away."

"Does that mean you won't be in to lunch, my dear?"

"It does, I'm afraid. And I'm supposed to be canvassing all afternoon. I'll see you at opening time this evening."

"Very well, sir," said Myra demurely.

Fen got into his car and drove to Sanford Morvel. As on the previous day, he found Wolfe and Humbleby just leaving the police station for lunch. They took him with them to the White Lion, where at a near-by table he saw Captain Watkyn still wilting beneath the inexorable pressure of Mr Judd's political opinions.

"Food first," said Wolfe. "Talk afterwards. We have revelations to make, of a sort. Unluckily they don't help us as regards the central problem, but they clear up a few loose ends. And talk about melodrama…"

He refused to say more until they were settled with their coffee in a secluded corner of the lounge. Then he produced the small, black steel box which he had taken from Jane Persimmons' room on the evening of her accident.

"We've opened this," he said, tapping it. "You remember I couldn't at first find the key? Well, it turned out that the hospital people had it—it was on a chain round the girl's neck. So I didn't, after all, have to commandeer a locksmith. What we found…'

He hesitated, glancing at Humbleby. And Humbleby, a match held to the end of his cheroot, said:

"Wolfe has doubts—and very proper ones, I'm sure—about whether we ought to communicate our discovery to you—not to you in particular, I mean, but to *any* outsider. The matter is a decidedly private one, and not to be bruited abroad. But I feel sure, and I've said as much to Wolfe, that we can rely on your discretion."

On this case, Fen reflected, his discretion was having to work overtime: first Bussy, then the Rector, and now this, whatever it might be. He made, however, noises of reassurance which Wolfe seemed to find acceptable.

"You'd better look through the contents of the box, sir," he said. "That'll explain the business as quickly as we could do."

With undisguised curiosity Fen acted on the suggestion. At first glance, the contents of the box were not startling—a number of letters, and, lying on top of them, a ring. But as Fen examined the ring more closely, his first insouciance vanished. It was of finely wrought gold, set with a ruby, and although Fen made no claim to the *expertise* of a lapidary, he could see that the stone was flawless, uncommonly large and beyond all question enormously valuable. The workmanship, he thought, was not modern; provisionally he assigned it to the seventeenth century.

He put the ring aside and took up the letters. There were about thirty-five of them, of varying lengths, and all except one were written by the same person. The notepaper had a crest for heading, and was yellowed at the edges; time had blanched the sprawling calligraphy and the unvarying signature "Robert"; the dates covered the period from August, 1924, to May, 1926.

And Fen, reading them through, was curiously moved; for they were love letters of a touching sincerity, re-enacting endearments and caresses long since left castaway in the vanished years; and the ghost of their dead passion stirred in his mind a primaeval bitter-sweet sense of transience. So for a while he was unaware of his prosaic environment, reliving, with a kind of compassion, the emotions of a man whom he had never known and would never know. And it was with something of reluctance that he eventually laid down the last of these letters and turned his attention to that other sheet, in a finer and more precise handwriting, which would explain and complete the tale.

It ran as follows:

April 7th, 1939

My Darling,
When you come to read this I shall be dead, and I'm afraid you may be very unhappy. Please don't be. Your father used to say that we should none of us mind death and dying nearly so much if we didn't insist on regarding life as a basically pleasant thing with unpleasant intervals, instead of as an unpleasant thing with intervals of happiness. And I think he was right. But I don't want to write a sermon, and you won't be wanting to read one. This letter is to tell you, Jane dear, about your father.
You've always supposed he died before you were

born, but that isn't true. He's alive now, I know, and perhaps still may be when you read this. But legally—I'm afraid I'm saying this terribly clumsily—legally you haven't got a father. I was never married to him.

Well, it's out. Please don't hate me too much, my darling. Somehow I've never been able to bring myself to tell you, and I know now I never shall. So I've taken this way, which I know is cowardly and may hurt you. Please forgive me. I don't know what to add, except that I hope that one day you'll be as marvellously happy as I was with Robert. Except for your sake, I haven't any regrets. And I'm leaving you his letters, because seeing how sincere and fine he was may help you to understand.

Your father is the present Lord Sanford. You'll want to know why he didn't marry me, and why he left me, and why we haven't kept in touch. But it's a long story, Jane dear, and one that's better forgotten. I know I was as much to blame as he was, so you mustn't feel resentful against him. He gives me a generous allowance, and I hope by the time you read this you'll be settled in life and able to forget about him. Perhaps it's wrong of me to tell you at all, I don't know. But one day you might find out by accident, and I should hate you to think that I'd been too ashamed and frightened to tell you myself.

Besides, there's something I want you to do for me. The ring with this is a Sanford family heirloom, given to the Second Earl by Charles I. Robert made me accept it, though I didn't want to, and made me promise to keep it as a memento of him as long as I lived. Well, I shall keep my promise, but after-

wards it must go back to the family, to Robert if he's still alive or to his son. Please do this for me, Jane. You must decide whether to take it yourself or whether just to send it. And remember it's worth a lot of money. For my sake don't feel you have a right to it, or that you have a claim on the family in any way. But I needn't have written that, because I know you won't.

I think that's all, darling. Now you know everything, forget everything and try not to blame me too much. You've been the best and most loving of daughters, and you ought to have had a better Mother. Remember I love you very much.

Your Mother

P.S. I'm afraid a daughter with so many prizes for English Composition won't think much of the style of this letter! It was terribly difficult to write—but you'll understand. God bless, my darling.

In silence Fen returned the letters and ring to the box, closed it, and handed it back to Wolfe.

"In spite of his 'generous allowance,'" he commented thoughtfully, "I can't say I feel very much enthusiasm for the late Lord Sanford...However, he's dead, and censoriousness is therefore rather a futile exercise."

Humbleby was contemplating his well-manicured nails. "So Jane Persimmons," he observed, "is a natural daughter of the last Lord Sanford, and a half-sister of the present one."

"The Rector," said Fen, "told me he thought her face familiar, and a resemblance between the two would account for that."

"There certainly is such a resemblance." Wolfe, with the

end of his index finger, was gently rotating a scallop-shell ash-tray on the table beside him. "I noticed it myself—but naturally I dismissed it as accidental...Well, we at least know why she came here. It was to return that ring. Which means, presumably, that her mother has just recently died."

"Without, it seems, first seeing the girl 'settled in life.'" Humbleby scowled at Wolfe's fidgeting, and after a moment took the ash-tray away from him on the pretext of stubbing out his cheroot. "I take it she had in mind—*has* in mind, I suppose I should say—some kind of—overture of friendship to Lord Sanford." And as he considered this feeble statement, Humbleby's scowl returned. "The situation is a delicate one," he asserted, even more feebly.

Neither Wolfe nor Fen was paying much attention to his remarks. Wolfe looked as if he might be ruminating some intricate problem of professional etiquette; and Fen was equating the rather Wilkie Collins-ish revelations of the black box with what he had observed of Jane Persimmons' behaviour prior to her accident. She had clearly been spying out the ground before deciding what would be the most reliable and dignified approach—which accounted for the curious little episode he had witnessed in the grounds of Sanford Hall. He felt considerable sympathy for her hesitation, since in returning the ring she would be obliged to explain her possession of it, and, if you are at all sensitive, the announcement to a strange young man that you are an illegitimate child of his father is not made without a good deal of preliminary soul-searching. A fictitious recital would, of course, be possible, but Fen suspected that Jane was not the sort of person who has recourse to fictitious recitals in order to avoid unpleasantness...In this aspect of the affair, only one minor mystery remained—the problem of why Jane had chosen to deliver the ring in person— with all the explanation which that necessarily involved—rather than send it anonymously by registered post. She was, it appeared, not likely to be well off, and in that case she might conceivably be hoping for some kind of financial assistance from Lord Sanford. But this hypothesis conflicted hopelessly with Fen's diagnosis of the girl's character; she would almost rather starve, he thought, than ask for money, and especially on that pretext. Well, the point was comparatively unimportant. No doubt when Jane was conscious again it would be cleared up.

"How was she when you left the hospital?" Fen demanded.

"Virtually out of danger, I gathered." Humbleby poured the tepid dregs of the coffee-pot into his cup and drank them noisily. "They're expecting her to recover consciousness at almost any time now—though even when she does they won't be encouraging her to talk for a few days."

"The attempt on her life," said Fen: "can that be linked up in any way with what we've just learned?"

"I don't see that it can," Humbleby answered, "because there's still no motive. If she were the rightful heir to the Sanford estates, or some rubbish of that sort, Lord Sanford might want her out of the way. But she clearly isn't...No, what *I'm* worried about is what we're going to *do*."

"*Do*?"

"About this knowledge we've acquired." Wolfe contemplated Fen in a slightly baleful fashion, as though it were he who had contrived this testing and involuted problem of discretion. "The fact that someone attacked this girl obviously doesn't entitle us to communicate to Lord Sanford facts of such an intimate and personal nature. On the other hand, since she was obviously going to tell him ultimately, it might be...well, humane, for us to do so."

"How is he likely to take it?" Fen enquired.

"From what I've seen of him," said Wolfe, "he seems a very decent young man."

"Then I'm for taking these letters and showing them to him."

"So, unofficially, am I," said Humbleby.

"So, as human being, am I," said Wolfe. "But as a police officer I know damned well I oughtn't to do anything of the kind. If anyone chose to make a stink about it, it would probably mean demotion for me."

"Lord Sanford would have reason to be grateful to you," Fen pointed out, "and the girl isn't the sort who raises a pother about things that are irrevocable."

Wolfe sighed. "All right, then. I'll risk it, and hope for the best. But I can't say," he added, "that it's a job I look forward to, subsequent repercussions apart."

"Then let me do it," said Fen.

"You, sir?" Wolfe spoke rather dubiously. "I'm not sure that that would improve matters—since by rights you, as an outsider, oughtn't to know anything about it at all."

But Humbleby supported Fen. "If the thing is going to be done," he said, "I suspect that Professor Fen would probably do it more tactfully than either you or I, Wolfe." Fen, who has a high opinion of his own tact but seldom hears it spontaneously recommended, made sounds of concurrence and gratification. "And I'm quite willing to take the entire responsibility on my own shoulders, since if a fuss *were* made the consequences would be less serious for me than for you. The police force, after all, isn't quite inhuman, and although one might be officially reproved, one would almost certainly be privately applauded...Besides, there's nothing to stop us saying, in the upshot, that we thought this business might be connected with the attack on the girl, and that therefore it had to be probed. And for all we know"—Humbleby leered at them with manifest disingenuousness—"such a connection may, in fact, exist."

"Is that settled, then?" Fen asked; and they nodded. "Good. I'll deal with it immediately." He took the steel box from Wolfe. "Oh, but before I go you'd better hear about the Rector's field-glasses." He briefly expounded these.

"Oh, come, sir," said Wolfe reproachfully. "It's a bit odd, I grant you, but I don't see how it can possibly link up with any of the other things."

"Nor, at the moment, do I," Fen admitted. "And quite possibly it doesn't. But I thought you might as well know."

Wolfe thanked him with the civil insincerity of a small boy who has anticipated an aeroplane for Christmas and been given a copy of the Bible, and Fen departed to inform Captain Watkyn that he would not be available for canvassing till after tea. Captain Watkyn received this information with a disapproval which was perceptibly enhanced when Mr Judd, who was still with him, insisted on taking Fen's place. He watched Fen's departure with the mingled piteousness and exasperation of a marooned sailor who sees the ship which might have salvaged him disappearing inexorably over the horizon.

Fen got into his car and drove to the dower-house of Sanford Hall.

(HAPTER EIGHTEEN

DIANA MERRION APPLIED a layer of polish to the off front mudguard of her car, picked up a soft cloth from the mudguard and began to rub vehemently. An observer—of that dispassionate sort which novelists summon to their assistance when direct description begins to pall—would have attributed her vehemence, on this uncommonly hot day, to a pride in workmanship. But such an observer, like the majority of his spectral and deluded kind, would have been seriously mistaken. It is true that in the normal way Diana bestowed a great deal of care on her Daimler, for she was a young woman to whom slovenliness was abhorrent; today, however, her energy derived not from devotion to good appearances, but from a simultaneous mental and physical discomfort. Her labours were the issue of exasperation; the gleaming chassis of the car bore witness to an unconquerable dissatisfaction.

Bodily unease was to be expected. The sun was beating down on the asphalt runway outside the small garage; the smallest movement raised clouds of weeks-old dust whose impact on the flesh was like the impact of itching-powder; and mosquitoes swooped predatorily whenever a reasonably safe and succulent bite was in prospect. Wasps, gorged and intoxicated with plums from the neighbourhood orchard, crawled laboriously but menacingly about, ready to ply their stings at the slightest touch. Diana's hair kept falling over one eye like a hot blanket; and every garment she wore felt soiled and scratchy. It was undeniably an idiotic day, and an idiotic time of the day, for exacting manual work.

Diana straightened up, and sombrely contemplated her distorted reflection in the polished metal of the mudguard. There were the door-handles and the windscreen still to do, but the door-handles and windscreen, she decided, could wait. Dirty, sweating and exhausted, she sat down on the running-board and began groping in the pocket of her slacks for a cigarette. But the pockets of one's slacks, when one is seated, tend to be tightly stretched against one's thighs and hence impermeable. With a little scream of impatience, Diana stood up and dragged the cigarettes out. She had sat down again, and gingerly extracted a cigarette with grubby fingers, before she remembered that the matches were in the other pocket of her slacks. She bounded up again and produced the box. It was empty. There were no matches in the cubby-holes of the car. There were no matches nearer at hand than the cottage where she lived, five hundred yards away. It was not worth walking that distance for the sake of a cigarette, however much one longed for one...Diana slumped down again on the running board. It was now, she found, physically impossible to return the cigarettes to her pocket. She put the carton on the running-board of the car, and since she had not closed it properly, all the cigarettes fell out onto the ground, and most of them rolled about under the car until they got settled in positions where it was impossible to reach them except by lying on one's stomach and rubbing one's hair—carefully washed only last night—against the mud on the underside of the running-board...

Diana made no attempt to retrieve them. Chin in hands, she sat ruminating moodily. Like most people, she laboured under the delusion that mental afflictions are always more unendurable than physical (though whether those who live in this faith would, in the event, choose a month's acute rheumatism rather than a month's serious anxiety is open to doubt); and therefore she blamed her present surliness not on her own folly in polishing a car under a torrid sun, but on the inexplicable erotic dilatoriness of Robert, Seventeenth Earl of Sanford. The local people, she knew, anticipated an early marriage; but in this they were disastrously over-sanguine. Not only was there no question of a marriage. There was no question, even of an Affair. And this it was that irked Diana, for with Robert, Seventeenth Earl of Sanford, she was deeply in love, and had been ever since the day when he had first summoned her to drive him from Sanford Hall to the railway station. They had on that occasion talked indifferently about indifferent topics. Sporadically, and at long intervals, they had repeated this innocuous social exercise. Then she had happened to mention that there wasn't a good place to bathe in the neighbourhood, and he had invited her to use the lake in the grounds of Sanford Hall whenever she felt inclined. And then one day he had come down and bathed with her, and while they dried themselves in the sun they had ceased talking indifferently about indifferent topics and started to quarrel fiercely about politics. And then they had taken to inviting one another to tea, and had continued to quarrel fiercely about politics. And that was absolutely all that had happened. For all she could tell, Robert was prepared to go on quarrelling fiercely about politics to all eternity. He had never put his arm around her; he had certainly never kissed her; he had never, as far as she was aware, even been human enough to glance at her legs—and they were worth more than a glance…So what in Hades was the matter with the man? She was sure (a little naïvely sure) that there wasn't another girl; vanity rebelled at believing that she didn't attract him in *any* way, even the merely physical; and he was clearly not the sort of man who is temperamentally antagonistic to women. The only conclusion she could reach, therefore, was that something in his upbringing had made him abnormally shy of the opposite sex. And if so, what ought she to do about it? She could not bear the thought of breaking with him altogether, but to go on as they were doing would be almost a worse martyrdom. And it seemed that a miracle would be required to make him regard her as anything more or other than a taxi-driver with Conservative views. Diana frowned anxiously. Should she take the initiative in some way? Well-bred young women do not throw themselves at the heads of young men—but that, of course, didn't matter a twopenny damn. The question *was*, whether such action would scare him off once and for all. And…

"Oh, hell," sighed Diana. "Damned if I know what to do. Why do I have to be so moronic as to fall in love with *him*, of all people? Just seeing him in the distance makes me feel as groggy as a schoolgirl at a James Mason picture."

Over this humiliating analogy, and the obscure but piercing shame of an unrequited affection, she brooded despondently and resentfully. Every second the sun seemed to grow hotter and more intolerable. Soon her thoughts reverted to the lake, and she decided that it would be a great deal more sensible to go and have a bathe rather than to continue to sit uncomfortably here, indulging in the shabby pleasures of self-pity. She had no commissions till after tea, and if anyone wanted the car for an emergency they'd just have to do without it…Diana roused herself, and being a provident girl grovelled for the scattered cigarettes. Then she drove along the quiet, deserted village street to her eighteenth-century cottage.

Here she undressed, energetically washed, put on a back-less white bathing dress with a clean white muslin frock on top of it, stuffed some underclothes and a bathing-cap into a handbag, hung a towel over one arm, emerged from the front door, re-entered it hurriedly to obtain matches, emerged again and drove to the grounds of Sanford Hall. The dower-house, a commodious place, stands some way away from the Hall itself, and Diana had to drive in through its gates to get to the lake. With a quickened pulse she looked about her to see if Robert might be visible somewhere out of doors, but he was not, and she drove on in slight though unacknowledged disappointment, the gravel drive taking her right through the gardens, where a courteous old gardener touched his cap as she passed, and out onto the rise of rough turf which overlooked the lake. Here she parked the car, and walked the remaining distance.

The lake was a small one, but ideal for bathing, since it was fed by a clean spring and discharged all its waste into a small tributary which issued in the river Spoor. Also, being out of sight of both the dower-house and the Hall, it was blissfully secluded—and if there was one type of humanity which Diana detested more than another, it was the type which stands or sits complacently and often concupiscently watching others swimming. The cool water sparkled in the sunlight. An unserviceable-looking rowboat with water in it slopped about in the ripples at the margin. And Diana, slipping off her frock and shoes and donning her bathing-cap, stood for a moment poised on the bank near it and then dived in.

The coolness of the water was sensual luxury of the most depraved kind. Savouring it, Diana swam slowly out to the centre of the lake and there lay on her back and floated, her eyes closed against the glaring afternoon light. From a confused but not unpleasant reverie she was roused by a cheerful shout from the bank, and, twisting over, opening her eyes and starting to swim again, she observed the Seventeenth Earl of

Sanford standing there, slim and delightful as an Adonis, his shirt open at the neck and his hands thrust into the pockets of shabby grey flannel trousers. A really determined girl, Diana reflected, would at this juncture pretend to be drowning, and by exhibiting maidenly gratitude after rescue make a subsequent romance inevitable. But really determined girls were presumably more practised than she in simulating aquatic disasters, and she had the feeling that as performed by her the manoeuvre would not carry much conviction. So she swam to the bank instead, clambered out, took off her bathing-cap and groped in her bag for a comb.

"Hello, Robert," she said. "You look as pleased as a dog with two tails. What's happened?"

He smiled charmingly at her. "It *is* nice to see you, Diana. I was rather hoping you'd turn up." With his unvarying courtesy he picked up her towel and handed it to her. "Something rather pleasant has happened, and I've been wanting all day to tell someone about it."

Diana experienced a stab of apprehension and misgiving; he wasn't—for heaven's sake!—going to tell her he was engaged to someone...? She rubbed her face determinedly with the towel. "Oh, what is it?" she asked, keeping her voice light and clear.

"It's my Finals at Oxford. I've just heard the result. I've got a First."

Diana looked up at his finely drawn, sunburnt face and with the utmost difficulty suppressed an impulse to burst into tears of thankfulness and relief. "But of course you have, Robert," she said. "I always knew you would."

He laughed, and she thought that she had never seen him so happy. "Then you knew more than I did."

"*Many* congratulations, Robert."

"Thank you, Diana...Look here, you're not doing anything this evening, are you?"

"I'm afraid I am. I've got several calls."

"Cancel them."

"But Robert—"

"Cancel them and come on a pub crawl with me. I want to celebrate, and I want to be thoroughly vulgar and conventional about it, and I want you with me. That is…" He hesitated, reddening a little. "If it wouldn't bore you."

Diana gulped, and only regained control of her voice by reminding herself that schoolgirls gulped at photographs of James Mason. "Oh, Robert, I'd love to," she said.

"Good. That's settled, then."

"Where and when do we meet?"

"I'll pick you up at your cottage about six-thirty. All right?"

"Lovely." And Diana, watching him, saw that almost imperceptibly his ebullience was beginning to subside. "Heavens, I know what's going to happen," she thought, suddenly panicky. "As soon as he cools down, he's going to start regretting the impulse that made him invite me out; and he's far too courteous to cancel the arrangement on that account, so we shall spend the whole evening drearily arguing about the government, like a couple of strangers in a railway compartment…Oh, Lord, am I *really* so unattractive?"

But all she said was: "I—I think I'd better get dressed now."

"Yes, of course you'd better," Robert assented, with as much haste as if he had suddenly perceived her to be completely nude. "I'll go away."

"No, you needn't do that. Just turn your back for a minute."

For the time being, however, there was to be no opportunity of getting dressed. As Diana spoke, a liveried butler of great stateliness appeared over the rise from the direction of the dower-house and glided up to them, bearing a visiting card on a salver. This he presented with impassive ceremony to Lord Sanford, who earnestly thanked him for his trouble.

"And you know, Houghton," he added, "there's no need, when you bring me a thing like this, to put it on a salver. That's only a relic of the days when the upper classes considered that things were soiled by servants touching them...There's a most interesting book"—Lord Sanford eyed his butler dubiously—"which tells you all about things like that."

"Would you by any chance be referring to Veblen's *Theory of the Leisure Class*, my lord?"

Lord Sanford was somewhat taken aback. "Well, yes, as a matter of fact I was. Have you read it?"

"Yes, my lord. And if I might venture the remark..." Houghton paused for the requisite permission.

"Of course, Houghton. This is a free country."

"I had not recently observed that, my lord...But about Veblen's book, what I was going to say was that its assertions, though plausible, are wholly unproved. And in my opinion, the same author's *The Engineers and the Price System* is a very much more important and illuminating work."

"Ah," said Lord Sanford rather unhappily. It was evident that he was not acquainted with this essay; he stared, embarrassed at the visiting card. "Let's see, who's this...Oh, Professor Fen. Perhaps"—he gazed indecisively about him—"you would ask Professor Fen if he would care to join us here."

"Very good, my lord."

"And Houghton, I've told you before that there's no need to address me as 'my lord.'"

"No, my lord."

"If there are to be distinctions in society, they should be based on achievements and not on birth."

Momentarily forgetting himself, Houghton made a low, longish, inflected sound which Diana interpreted as "lotof-bloodynonsense." Then, recovering, "Quite so, my lord," he observed, bowed obsequiously and departed. Lord Sanford gazed after him in despair.

"I never know what to make of Houghton," he said ruefully. "Or the other servants, for that matter. You'd think they'd be glad to be rid of all these…these emblems of servility, but in fact they seem determined to stick to them at all costs."

Diana suppressed a desire to giggle. "But my dear Robert," she said, "hasn't it yet occurred to you that they may actually *enjoy* what you call 'the emblems of servility'?"

"Well, that's even worse. A system which makes people enjoy being servile ought to be abolished."

"I didn't say they enjoyed being servile. They aren't servile. The only servile person in the house is you."

"You may be right about that," Lord Sanford admitted after some thought. "But all the same, Diana, it's disgraceful that five people should devote their whole lives to looking after me, and doing things for me which I could quite well do for myself. As you know, I've tried to get rid of them, but they just won't go."

"Oh, Robert, of course they won't go; they're on velvet," Diana pointed out. "And it just isn't true to say they devote their whole lives to looking after you. Most of their time's spent doing something quite different."

"What do you mean?"

"Looking after each other, of course. It's a most luxurious co-operative arrangement, and if they went off and took independent jobs it'd collapse altogether."

"Yes, I see *that*," said Lord Sanford, who was an intellectually honest young man. "It *is* a good arrangement. But it'd work equally well—better, in fact—if I wasn't involved in it all."

"On the contrary, it wouldn't work at all. Someone's got to pay them the salaries they live on."

"Yes, Diana, but look here…"

And it was at this point that, quite without premonition, sudden exasperation overwhelmed Diana—exasperation not with Lord Sanford's views on servants, but with the fact that they were back again in the old groove.

"Robert!" she interrupted.

"Yes, Diana?"

"Kiss me, please."

For an instant his face was a study in stupefaction. And then his expression changed to one of such relief and delight that Diana's heart sang.

He did what was required.

Their mumbled endearments were too extrinsically futile to be worth reproducing here. And their first contact gave them such mutual satisfaction that they immediately repeated it, at much greater length.

"Of course you'll marry me," said Lord Sanford with an air of surprise.

"Of course," Diana agreed. "Tell me, darling, are you frightened of young women?"

"Terrified."

"I'll try to let you down lightly...Darling, what are you going to do next?"

Lord Sanford made certain suggestions.

"No, not *that*," said Diana, blushing slightly. "I mean, now you've got your First."

"I think," said Lord Sanford gravely, "that as soon as we're married it would be a good idea for us to go off and be cook and gardener to a Trades Union official. For the Cause, you understand."

"Oh, darling, that would be heavenly. Well, fairly heavenly."

"It would be torture of the most refined and abominable sort," said Lord Sanford with conviction. "Actually, I shall try for a Fellowship at Oxford. There are lots of Socialist Fellows. There's Cole, and there's—"

"Cole will be sufficient for now. Kiss me again."

"Professor Fen—"

"Damn Professor Fen," said Diana unjustly. Lord Sanford kissed her again.

They were still at it when Fen came in sight. He did not discreetly retire, but bore relentlessly down on them, with Jane Persimmons' box under his arm, like a dragon making for a defenceless and succulent child. Having sent his card, he felt he had given all the warning of his approach which decency required, and he was not prepared to skulk about until they were in a posture to receive him. He was only five yards off when they became aware of him, and hurriedly disengaged themselves.

"Oh, Professor Fen," said Diana unintelligently. "It's you."

"So it is," said Lord Sanford, not much less inanely. "Good afternoon, sir."

Fen shook him by the hand, which was still damp from contact with Diana's undried body. "I hope," he said urbanely, "that I don't intrude?"

"Good Lord, no." The Seventeenth Earl spoke with such heartiness as to suggest that Fen's absence had been the only flaw in an otherwise perfect afternoon. "Not in the least. I hope you've come to tea."

"That's very kind. But first, I'm afraid, there's rather an important matter I want to discuss with you."

"Yes, of course." Lord Sanford glanced at Diana. "Perhaps I ought to tell you that Diana—Miss Merrion—has just consented to marry me: so from now on, anything that concerns me concerns her, too."

Fen looked at them benignantly. "Well, I think that's a very good scheme," he said. "Getting married, I mean. Of course, it mostly doesn't work out very well," he added by way of encouragement, "but yours may be an exceptional case. I'll send you a wedding present, if I remember. But as regards my errand here"—he became more serious—"it might perhaps be the easier way, my lord, if you were to hear of it first and then to tell Diana subsequently."

"If you really think so—"

"On the whole, I do."

"Well, you can talk while I get dressed," said Diana, "and afterwards we can all have tea together."

"Or a drink," said Fen, who never hesitated to make his requirements known. "Your engagement calls, I fancy, for a drink, and even if it didn't I should still want one."

"A drink, of course," Lord Sanford agreed good-naturedly. "And now, sir..."

Diana retired into a convenient thicket, and the two men strolled slowly along the lake-side. "There's no need for me to do any talking," said Fen. "The contents of this box explain themselves. All I need say is that the box is the property of a girl called Jane Persimmons."

"You mean, sir, the girl who had that accident, and whom someone tried to kill?"

"Yes. I'll leave you to it, if I may, and stroll round the grounds."

When he returned some twenty minutes later, Diana, re-clothed, was sitting with Lord Sanford at the lake's edge, and both were thoughtful.

"I've told my *fiancée*," said Lord Sanford.

"Quite so," Fen murmured. "Very proper. Of course you may rely on my discretion, and on the discretion of the police. Do you consider we did right in letting you know?"

"Certainly you did right." Lord Sanford spoke with that touching earnestness which belongs exclusively to the young. "My father...Well, I knew he hadn't been faithful to my mother, but I never dreamed there was a child." Fen noted with pleasure that his calmness was not the calmness of cynicism. "Diana and I want to do everything for Jane that we can. We hope she'll come and live with us."

"You'll have to be extremely tactful about it," Fen warned him. "From what I've seen of her, she's an uncommonly sensitive girl. There must be no suspicion that you're offering charity."

Lord Sanford nodded in sober agreement. And Diana said:

"I knew all along there was some mystery about her, and she's so like you, Robert, that I was passionately keen to find out what the mystery was…I was going to mention the resemblance to Professor Fen at the time of her accident, but then I thought it might be just my imagination, so I didn't."

"And how is she?" Lord Sanford enquired of Fen.

"Recovering fast, I understand."

"Well, I shall see to it, of course, that everything possible is done for her. Diana and I have agreed to go down to the hospital and see her, as soon as we possibly can. But this attempt on her life…" Lord Sanford glanced at Fen in mute perplexity.

"It's connected with the other deaths. She knows something about them—without, in all probability, knowing that she knows. As soon as they're cleared up, she'll be safe enough."

"Shortly, it may be. I have the ghost of a sensible idea about them, which is more than I've had so far."

"Tell us," said Diana.

"Not yet, if you don't mind."

"Champagne might melt him, Robert."

"Whether it does or not, we'll have some."

Fen accompanied them back to the dower-house. They were an amiable couple, he thought; they would like Jane Persimmons and she would like them. In that direction all would probably be well. He dismissed the matter from his mind and fell to considering the circumstances of Bussy's death.

(HAPTER NINETEEN

By SOME CHICANERY into which Fen did not feel impelled to enquire, Captain Watkyn had forestalled the Labour and Conservative parties in procuring, for the final public meeting on the following night, the best hall which Sanford Morvel had to offer; and it was tolerably well filled. Enthroned at the centre of the platform, and pretending to listen while Mr Judd droned away about the evils of the party political system, Fen contemplated with contentment the speech which he proposed to make. His decision had not been rashly taken; he is, on the whole, a kindly man, and he was well aware that his action would give pain to the small band of his loyal supporters. But this consideration was as a feather on a scale whose opposite pan was weighted by his determination not to be elected and by his anxiety to cleanse a mind which he felt irreparably fouled by the week's political activities. Mental antisepsis and political ruin should, he had determined, be accompanied by a single unprecedented act. And although most probably he would not be returned to Parliament in any case, any lingering risk of such an eventuality must be abolished once and for all; the Stewardship of the Chiltern Hundreds, he had discovered, was not to be had merely for the asking, and he was no longer prepared to chance being immured in the intellectual vacuum of Westminister for even so short a period as three years. He sat mobilising his wits against this self-inflicted peril.

Thus it was that, when at last Mr Judd fell silent, Fen got to his feet and stood for a moment surveying the rows of politely expectant faces below him with a satisfaction such as he had not experienced in his whole lifetime. And the survey completed, the banquet of consternation savoured in anticipation, he removed the safety-pin from his grenade.

"It is often asserted," he said, "that the English are unique among the nations for their good sense in political matters. In actual fact, however, the English have no more political good sense than so many polar bears. This I have proved in my own person. For some days past I have been regaling this electorate with projects and ideas so incomparably idiotic as to be, I flatter myself, something of a *tour de force*. Into what I have said no gleam of reason has been allowed to intrude; and I can think of scarcely a single error, however ancient and obscure, which I have failed to propagate. Some, it is true, have cavilled at my twaddle; but their objection has been to its superficies, and not to its inane basic principles, which have included, among other laughable notions, the idea that humanity progresses, and that fatuous corruption of the Christian ethic which asserts that everyone is responsible for the well-being of everyone else. Such dreary fallacies as these, expounded by myself, have been swallowed hook, line and sinker. And I am bound to conclude that this proven obtuseness is not unrepresentative of the British people as a whole, since their predilection for putting brainless megalomaniacs into positions of power stems, in the last analysis, from an identical vacuity of the intellect."

He paused, regarding his audience benignly. A dreadful hush had fallen, but as yet they seemed too stupefied with surprise to make audible protest.

"What is referred to as the political good sense of the British," Fen continued, "resolves itself upon investigation into the simple fact that until quite recently the British have been politically apathetic, paying as little attention to the bizarre junketings of their elected legislators as they decently could. It is this which accounts for the smoothness of our nation's development in comparison with the other countries of Europe; and our fabled spirit of compromise—now virtually extinct— has derived from nothing more obscure or complicated than a general indifference as to the issue of whatever controversy may have been in hand; though we, of course, have in our vanity ascribed it to tolerance. Propaganda, however, has altered all that, and politics nowadays engender heat, dismay, fury and a variety of other discreditable emotions in every section of the populace. We are forever at each other's throats; the safety-valve of our apathy is twisted and broken beyond repair. Only here and there does it survive, and I am happy to note that this constituency is one of its last strongholds. I congratulate this constituency on the fact. And I strongly advise this constituency, when confronted with reformers-by-compulsion who assert that it is every man's duty to take an interest in politics, to kick those gentry downstairs. For such an asseveration there is no single justification to be found, whether in morality, metaphysics, expediency or sense. Do not allow yourselves to be cajoled into supposing that political apathy is dangerous. Dictators such as Hitler, Mussolini and Stalin are raised to power not by apathy, but by mass fanaticism. That, darlings, is the danger, but you are so busy gaping up at me and wondering if I have gone out of my mind that I could talk for a week without convincing you of it. I do not intend to talk for a week. English political fanaticism is fast growing to a spate, and nothing that I or anyone else can do or say will check it now.

"I shall now tell you the reason why fanaticism of this sort is so attractive to humankind. A contemporary French writer—whose name I shall not mention, since you are probably too stupid either to recognise it or to remember it—has pointed out with unanswerable logic that men adopt ideas not because it seems to them that those ideas are true, or because it seems to them that those ideas are expedient, but because those ideas satisfy a basic emotional need of their nature. Now what emotion—I ask you—provides the chief motive power of the politically obsessed? You do not answer, because you have never given the matter a moment's thought. But were you to do so, even you might dimly perceive that the reply to my question is the monosyllable *hate*. Never forget that political zealots are people who are over-indulging their emotional need of hatred. They have, of course, their 'constructive' programmes, but it is not these which supply the fuel for their squalid engines; it is the concomitant attacks, upon a class, a system, a personality; it is the lust to defame and destroy. Let no such men be trusted. That they have landed themselves, here and hereafter, in the most arid of all the hells is a circumstance which I must confess does not greatly distress me, and with that spiritual aspect of the matter I do not propose to deal. However, certain important practical consequences emerge, and I shall illustrate one of them by means of a fable which I have cleverly invented for the purpose.

"There lived in a forest three foxes, named Shadrach, Meshach and Abednego. Shadrach had a fine suit of clothes and was immensely proud of it. Meshach had a portable gramophone and some records of dance music, to which he was greatly addicted. Abednego had a hogshead of ale, replenished monthly, with which he fortified himself against the manifold horrors of existence. In this fashion they co-existed for a long period, troubling little about each other. But there came a day when Meshach, communing with his soul in the forest to the accompaniment of a tango, discovered for the first time the obscene pleasures of righteous indignation. And having discovered them, he went to Abednego and communicated them to him, saying: 'Shadrach has a fine suit of clothes, and we have not. It is not just or equitable that Shadrach should be thus privileged.' So they went together to Shadrach, overpowered him and took his fine suit of clothes away from him. But as there was only one fine suit of clothes and they could not agree which of them was to wear it, they burned it. So then nobody had a fine suit of clothes.

"And a year or so passed, and Abednego, whose indignation was more righteous than ever, went to Shadrach and said: 'Meshach has a portable gramophone and a number of records of dance music, and we have not. It is not just or equitable that Meshach should be thus privileged.' So they went together to Meshach, over-powered him and took his portable gramophone and his records of dance music away from him. But as there was only one portable gramophone and they could not agree which of them was to use it, they threw it into a pond. So then nobody had a portable gramophone.

"And a year or so passed, and Meshach went to Shadrach and said: 'Abednego has a hogshead of ale and we have not. It is not just or equitable that Abednego should be thus privileged.' So they went together to Abednego, over-powered him and took his hogshead of ale away from him. But as there was not enough to be shared between them, they poured it all into a river. So then nobody had anything, and they were all so angry with one another that they quarrelled, came to blows, and thus fell an easy prey to a number of cannibal foxes which descended on them from the East and tore them limb from limb.

"This admirable tale is of course only a simplified version of what is at present going on in this country, but it mirrors the essential facts. My foxes desired that in the upshot there should be enough gramophones and ale and clothes for all of them. But they hated one another so much that the scheme was impossible to put into effect, and it is my salutary view that they deserved all they got.

"I intended to talk for a long time about the effects which endemic envy and hatred, masquerading as a public-spirited interest in politics, are producing in this country; but I now find that I am tired of looking at your rather plain faces, so I shall not do so. In conclusion I may as well add, however, that if you take my advice you will not go to the polls at all tomorrow. The politicians will not like this, because your indifference will be an affront to their sordid trade; but you must not let that worry you.

"That is all I have to say.

"Now go home and think about it."

And with a paralysed silence for valediction, Fen strode off the platform.

❋ ❋ ❋

An hour later Captain Watkyn, almost in tears, found him drinking beer and talking cricket on the lawn of the Fish Inn. A decorative sunset over-arched the scene.

"What got into you?" wailed Captain Watkyn. "For God's sake, what got into you?"

"I was easing my soul," said Fen placidly.

"But look here, old boy, you can't have *meant* all that."

"Some of it I meant. Of course, the British people is not a quarter as stupid as I made out; the delights of invective rather ran away with me there. What's the reaction?"

"I'm surprised you weren't lynched," said Captain Watkyn. "I'm surprised they didn't throw things," he added as a rather less impressive alternative. "Well, they just shuffled out, muttering among themselves; that's all that happened. But you can take it from me, old boy, you've queered your pitch properly."

"Do you really think so?"

"You'll be lucky now," said Captain Watkyn with emphasis, "if you get a single vote."

And Fen smiled.

CHAPTER TWENTY

THAT FEN'S SPEECH should have fallen victim to a newspaper conspiracy of silence is not really surprising. Sub-editors stared incredulously at it and enquired of aggrieved reporters whether they were drunk or just plain demented. Managing editors communicated hurriedly with the proprietors of their sheets, and were instructed not to mention the affair. There was no political capital to be made out of it from any angle, and although some account of it might have been published had Fen been certifiably insane, this tempting possibility was unanimously rejected by those who were on the spot. The device of total oblivion was all that remained.

So much Fen had himself anticipated. What he had not anticipated at all was the perverse local reaction to his words. His first intimation of this came from Mr Judd on the following morning, the Saturday. Fen had risen late; and when, about mid-day, he drifted into the bar of the Inn, he found Mr Judd perched on a stool there, watching the graceful movements of Jacqueline with the stony intentness of a cat watching a bird.

Fen had not been looking forward to meeting Mr Judd; though
he knew that Mr Judd's devotion to the cause of independence
in politics was almost wholly egotistical, he none the less felt
guilty of a profound and far-reaching betrayal. He was the
more surprised, therefore, that Mr Judd should greet him with
such obviously unfeigned cordiality.

"My dear Fen, this *is* a pleasure. Come and have a drink.
What is it to be?"

"Well, whisky."

"A large whisky, Jacqueline, my dear…Fen, I must congratulate you on your speech last night."

"Congratulate me?" Fen repeated incredulously. "Of
course. It was delicious."

"Are you sure, Judd, that you understood what I was
saying?"

Mr Judd chuckled as he paid for the whisky. "Certainly I
did. You made a savage attack on the British people and proph-
esied for them a future of irremediable disaster."

"But you can't possibly *approve* of my having done that."

"I don't agree with you," said Mr Judd more seriously, "but
that doesn't alter the fact that it was enormous fun."

Fen was dismayed. "Fun?" he said.

"Just that. Do you know the essays of H. L. Mencken?"

"I'm inordinately fond of them. I can't subscribe to half he
says, but the way he says it is masterly."

"That's what I mean about your speech. Naturally, I was
startled at first, but I soon settled down to enjoy myself."

"*But I was being deliberately insulting.*"

"Agreed. But you must remember that the insults were
more or less impersonal. What's more, it was obvious that you
were thoroughly happy, and happiness is infectious. What's
more, very few people took you seriously."

"Are you saying that they regarded the whole thing as a
sort of music-hall turn?"

"Well, in a way. It's difficult to explain, I'm afraid, but there's a queer instinct in people which makes them rather enjoy being cheerfully and exaggeratedly abused. That's why hell-fire preachers are so popular. And even when you're being offensive, my dear fellow, you continue to radiate a most seductive personal charm."

"Charm," Fen muttered, much disgruntled.

"Of course, some people were angry. But a quite surprising number weren't. It was all such a *relief,* you see, compared with what they expected. Oh, dear, I'm explaining this very badly. But the fact itself remains: you may have antagonised a few people, but your catharsis has probably gained you more votes than you've lost. Be honest: wouldn't you vote for a candidate who had the courage to make a speech like that?"

"Well, I'm damned," said Fen in deep disgust.

❁ ❁ ❁

In the afternoon he drove in to Sanford Morvel to see Wolfe.

"Well, Professor Fen, you've certainly caused a sensation," Wolfe greeted him. "I wish I'd been there."

"Look here, Wolfe, is it true that people actually didn't *mind* what I said last night?"

"Oh, the stuffier folk are up in arms about it, as you'd expect. But lots of your audience loved it. One man I talked to said he'd been longing all his life for a political bloke to get up on his hind legs and say something like that. This man was going to vote Labour—in fact, he came to your meeting to heckle—but he's decided now to vote for you instead."

"Good God," said Fen indistinctly.

After a few more enquiries he reluctantly abandoned the topic and got down to business. During the night he had reached a definite conclusion regarding the identity of the murderer X; and since there were loose ends to be tidied up, and the process might take time, he wished to make sure that this person did not escape from the neighbourhood, or make a further attempt to kill Jane Persimmons, before he was in a position to get an arrest-warrant. With this end in view, he communicated certain opinions to Wolfe. And Wolfe was dumbfounded.

"Good Lord, sir," he said. "I never dreamed...Then I take it you want me to keep an eye on her."

"Just give me twenty-four hours," said Fen. "That should be enough."

He drove back to the Inn and sought out Myra.

"Myra," he said, "I want you, please, to remember everything you can about the afternoon Jane Persimmons had her accident."

"I'll try, my dear. Where do you want me to start?"

"Let's say five o'clock. With as much detail as you can manage."

"Well, at five o'clock I was having tea in my room with Jackie, and Jackie was mending a ladder in her second-best nylons for the dance we were going to in the evening."

"Was Jane Persimmons about?"

"I think she was in her room, my dear, though I wouldn't absolutely swear to it."

"And Bussy—Crawley, that's to say?"

"He was out, I know that."

"Right. Go on."

Myra frowned with effort of recollection. "Well, nothing happened that I can remember till the Superintendent arrived from Sanford Morvel. That'd be about twenty past. I gave him a cup of tea, and he sat down and we chatted, friendly like. He'd had complaints we weren't closing dead on time, and I don't say we always do, but he hasn't any more use for these ruddy puritans than I have, so he just warned me, quite pleasantly, to be a bit more careful in future, or he'd have to take official notice of it. Then he got up and went at—let's see, it'd be just before six. Only he didn't drive off straightaway: he tinkered about a bit inside the bonnet of his car."

"Yes, never mind him," said Fen. "What did you do?"

"I opened up the bar and—no, wait, I didn't do that straight away. The girl, that's Jane Persimmons, hadn't said if she was going to be in for dinner, so I went up to her room to find out."

"You were alone?"

"No, Jackie was with me. She was going to change."

"So you knocked"—Fen wanted minutiae at this stage—"on Jane's door."

"Yes, I did, and opened it straight away without waiting for an answer." Myra was quick-witted enough to understand what had motivated Fen's prompting. "The girl was standing by the window where the dressing-table is, and when I looked in she put something quickly into a drawer, as though she didn't want me to see what it was."

"And you *didn't* see what it was?"

"I'm afraid not, my dear. And then—"

"Just a moment. Can you remember exactly what time it was?"

Myra smiled her worldly and charming smile. "Oh, I'm the perfect witness, sir. Just as I knocked on the door the Church clock was striking six. I know that because of course the bar's due to open at six, and I was keeping an eye on the time."

"Good," said Fen. "And what happened after Jane put whatever it was into the drawer?"

"I asked if she'd be in to dinner and she said yes, and she was going out for a walk first. So she picked up her bag and came out on the landing and shut the door behind her, and we went downstairs together."

"Was Jacqueline with you all this time?"

"Yes, she was. *She* came downstairs too, because I suddenly remembered the potatoes weren't peeled, and I asked her to do it because I had to open the bar, and it's a messy job so she didn't want to change till it was finished."

"And then?"

"Then the girl left us at the bottom of the stairs and went out. I saw she stopped and talked to the Superintendent for a minute or two, but I don't know what it was about. She set off along the road and Jackie went into the kitchen and I went down to the cellar to put on a new barrel of mild. About five minutes after that I heard your Scotland Yard friend shouting for me, and it turned out he was leaving and wanted his bill in a hurry. So I gave it him and took his money, and went and opened the bar. And a bit later Diana drove him to the station in her taxi, and after that nothing happened till you came in and told me about the accident."

"Good," said Fen. "That's as far as we need go. Now, about this dance you and Jacqueline visited in Sanford Morvel: what time did you arrive there?"

"About a quarter to eleven, my dear."

"And you left when?"

"One a.m. prompt. 'Goodnight, Sweetheart,' 'God Save the King' and out you go."

"And did either you or Jacqueline leave the dance at any time?"

"No, my dear. It wasn't us that knifed the detective."

"I didn't imagine it was," said Fen, smiling, "but I believe in stopping loopholes."

"Then you're beginning to see daylight?"

"Lots of it."

"I wish," said Myra wistfully, "that I'd been at your meeting last night."

"Oh, to hell with my meeting," said Fen crossly, his personal misgivings returning in full spate. "I wish I'd just withdrawn my candidature and left it at that."

Myra was greatly surprised. "But don't you *want* to be elected, my dear?"

"Not now. I did at first, but not now."

"Well, if that's so, you've wasted a devil of a lot of money."

"Yes," said Fen impenitently. "Oh, there's one other thing I was wanting to ask, Myra. Was Jane Persimmons away from the Inn earlier on the day of her accident?"

"Yes, my dear. She wasn't here for lunch, and I don't think she came back till about four."

"Did you see her come in?"

"No, I didn't. I only heard her. Is it important?"

"Not essential. It might possibly have confirmed what's already obvious...Well, thank you, Myra."

"You're welcome, my dear."

Samuel appeared. He was clutching, by the neck, a scrawny chicken which to judge by olfactory criteria had been dead far too long.

"Urrggh," he said disgustedly on perceiving Fen.

"You may get your peacocks yet," said Fen encouragingly to Myra. He left her to contend alone with Samuel's disreputable bargaining, and was pleased if not surprised when Jacqueline, located in the kitchen, corroborated her narrative in every detail.

Leaving the Inn, he encountered Mr Beaver uselessly examining his nugatory blueprint. The destruction was by this time far-reaching; dust seeped perpetually under the doors, like smoke in a burning house; doomed islets in a rising flood, Fen's room and Myra's and Jacqueline's and the bar were alone untouched. And now it seemed that the bar, the very heart of the Inn, was about to succumb.

"We've got to take that beam away from the ceiling," said Mr Beaver. "That's going to be a job."

"I think, you know," Fen ventured, "that it might be rather

a dangerous thing to do. The beam is probably an organic part of the house's structure."

"It'll be all right," said Mr Beaver with distinct surliness. Myra's uncomplimentary estimate of his staying-power had apparently been accurate.

Fen devoted the next twenty-four hours to establishing beyond all possible doubt that Myra and Jacqueline had been uninterruptedly dancing, on the previous Monday night, between eleven and one. Such thoroughness is foreign to his nature, but in this instance he thought it worth while. Finally, towards mid-day on the Sunday, he visited the hospital and ascertained from a number of doctors and nurses that, by no conceivable eventuality could Jane Persimmons have recovered consciousness between the moment of her accident and the following Thursday afternoon; and the suggestion that unconsciousness might have been feigned was met with a contemptuous and unqualified negative. Jane, he learned, was decidedly better; Diana and Lord Sanford had three times tried to see her, but for the moment it was desirable that she should do no talking. There was good hope of a rapid and complete recovery.

So that, Fen reflected, was that.

He drove to the Town Hall for the result of the poll.

❀ ❀ ❀

Throughout the previous day the inhabitants of the neighbourhood had trickled to the polling-booths. At six o'clock the polling-booths had closed and a count had been begun. By nine o'clock a recount was in progress, by nine the following morning a second recount, and by eleven a third. This conscientiousness was explained by the eventual verdict, which was as follows:

Gervase Fen (Independent), 1,207
Bertram Strode (Conservative), 1,206

Aloysius Wither (Labour), 1,206
Independent majority, 1

"*Damn*," said Fen.

Strode and Wither shook his hand with unconcealed resentment. He made a brief and unenthusiastic speech to a small crowd which had gathered to hear the announcement; and although they vaguely cheered, they were clearly disappointed by its conventionality.

"Congratulations, old boy, and may your shadow never grow less," said Captain Watkyn. "I told you all along that your final speech would get you a lot of votes, and so it has. Not a very big majority perhaps, but in my opinion that's because we never got that blasted loudspeaker van back on the road...I tell you what, we'll have a drink on this."

Fen looked at his watch. It was half past mid-day. "There's something I must deal with first," he said. "I'll meet you at the Fish Inn in about an hour."

"Right-oh," said Captain Watkyn agreeably.

Fen went to the police station. But the Superintendent, he was told, had driven in to Sanford Angelorum. Detective-Inspector Humbleby might possibly be at the White Lion.

Detective-Inspector Humbleby was at the White Lion. He sat alone in the bar, smoking a cheroot and drinking an atrocious decoction of sherry and draught beer. Fen waved his congratulations peremptorily aside and expounded his findings. As he talked, Humbleby's expression grew incredulous, and he protested vehemently; but presently, under the impulsion of hard, unarguable logic, his normally amiable face grew hard and unforgiving.

"You're perfectly right, of course," he said at last. "And I ought to have been able to work it out myself."

"You hadn't the advantage," Fen pointed out, "of talking to Jane Persimmons."

"No, but I knew all about her, and that should have been enough."

"You can act now?"

"Oh, certainly. The evidence is ample."

"What about a warrant?"

"I can get that at once."

They drove up to the Fish Inn at half past one exactly. The bar was already a ruin, its huge centre-beam extracted and propped perilously against an outside wall; but there was a small knot of people drinking on the lawn. Mr Judd was there, hovering about Jacqueline like a moth round a flame; Diana and Lord Sanford were there, shamelessly holding hands; Myra was there; Captain Watkyn was there; Wolfe was there. And Humbleby strode across to them, with Fen and a weighty police constable in his wake. They looked at his face, and their greetings died in their throats. He said:

"Edward Austin Wolfe, it is my duty to warn you that anything you say may be taken down and used in evidence hereafter. I now arrest you on a charge of murdering Detective-Inspector Charles Bussy by means of a knife at Sanford Angelorum on September fifteenth, 1947."

CHAPTER TWENTY-ONE

OF WHAT IMMEDIATELY followed, no lucid and reliable account is to be had. Fen's own subsequent statement, that he made a gallant and single-handed attempt to fell Wolfe, has been repudiated by the other witnesses, who assert unanimously that he did not so much as move. Wolfe, however, did move; by the time Humbleby's pistol was out of his pocket he had dragged Jacqueline in front of him as a shield, and was backing away with her towards his car, which stood outside in the road. For a sufficient time the incident paralysed their common sense; though it might not be possible to shoot at Wolfe, there was still no objection to tackling him bodily; and yet by an irrational quirk of the mind they held back, feeling themselves powerless, until he was almost at the car. Humbleby was the first to regain the capacity for rational thought.

"After him, damn you!" he shouted; and began running.

Urged on by Captain Watkyn, from a position well to the rear, the other men followed suit. But it was too late. Wolfe flung Jacqueline savagely aside and leaped into the car. It started at a touch, and in another moment was away. Humbleby fired two shots at the tyres, but without effect.

"I never was much good with these things," he said resignedly. "Come on."

He and Fen rushed for the car in which they had arrived. So also did the constable, but he was pushed out again with a bellowed injunction to send out a general alarm. The last Fen saw of the astonished group at the Inn was Mr Judd solicitously but needlessly brushing Jacqueline's skirt with the palm of his hand; Fen decided that Jacqueline must be devoid of nerves, for she looked as pleasantly equable and unperturbed as ever.

Wolfe had not achieved a long start, and there seemed little chance of his eluding them. He turned up the road which led to the railway station, and beyond that to Sanford Condover; evidently he was not going to risk being stopped in Sanford Morvel. The Wythendale direction would probably have suited him best of all, but his car had been facing the wrong way, and turning it had of course been out of the question. They bucketed along, momentarily losing sight of their quarry behind the bends of that winding lane, but never, since there were no side turnings, in danger of losing him altogether. The scene of Fen's first encounter with the lunatic flashed past—and by this time it was abundantly clear to him that Humbleby's inefficiency with a pistol was surpassed only by his inefficiency in driving an automobile; the speed at which they were travelling no doubt involved some risk, but not, surely, *all this* risk; most of it derived unquestionably from the fact that Humbleby was of that order of drivers who, having put the wheel over, wait until they have entirely rounded a corner before beginning to move it back again.

"Is there much point in our chasing him like this?" Fen demanded apprehensively. "He's almost certain to be picked up somewhere."

"This is a personal issue," said Humbleby grimly. "He killed one of my colleagues and I propose to do everything I possibly can towards ensuring that he's hanged."

"We'll both be dead if you go on driving like this."

Humbleby was much astonished, but the off wheels of the car, lurching over a high grass verge, distracted his attention from whatever defensive reply he might have contemplated making. Fen sat back resignedly and thought about his sins.

Three images of Nemesis presided over Wolfe's eventual fate, and now the first of them confronted him. The abysmal Shooter, whose fallen tree lay half across the lane near the station, had chosen this afternoon to set about removing it. Horses were there to drag its roots from the hedge; a cart was there for its ultimate removal; Shooter and his sons were there, quarrelling lengthily about ways and means. At the moment when Wolfe's car arrived at the spot, their united efforts had so far shifted the tree as to cause it to block the lane not partially but entirely. There was no getting past it.

But by a delusive and temporary stroke of luck there was a gate into which it was possible for Wolfe to back his car. He turned, driving back, since no other course was open to him, in the direction whence he had come. Humbleby and Fen heard his approach—and since they were not yet in sight of Shooter and his barricade, it did not for an instant occur to them that it might be he. Humbleby squeezed the car in against the hedge: Fen sat bolt upright, histrionically invoking the protection of St. Christopher. And Wolfe's car, rounding the bend ahead, scraped past them within two inches.

"God damn and blast him to hell," said Humbleby.

His turning, though by no means so rapid and efficient as Wolfe's was somehow accomplished. The chase proceeded, in a reverse direction, and the chattering, excited group outside the Fish Inn—swollen, now, by an admixture of villagers—stood suddenly petrified with amazement as the two cars came in view again. Fen caught a fleeting glimpse of their stupefaction as he was swept past; then, his gaze back on the road in front, he saw that Wolfe was turning into the lane which led up past the Rectory and so along the twelve miles to Wythendale.

Here it was that the second image of Nemesis awaited him. Along the exact centre of the lane, its head bandaged but its homing instinct unimpaired, trotted the non-doing pig, making resolutely for the Fish Inn. Wolfe saw it and—the training of a lifetime triumphing unexpectedly over his desperate lust of self-preservation—swerved to avoid it. So swerving, one of the front wheels of his car jarred against the grassy bank, and the engine died. The self-starter whined long and petulantly and unavailingly. As Fen and Humbleby drove up, Wolfe scrambled out of his car, and after glancing wildly about him, ran in at the Rectory gate.

They followed. The Rector, peaceably scrutinising his flower-beds on the way out to Sunday School, found himself without warning precipitated to the ground. Panic-stricken, Wolfe made for the front door, ran through it, slammed it behind him. A moment more, and Humbleby had scrambled in after him through an open downstairs window.

Fen paused to help the Rector to his feet, and in a few words informed him of what was going on. From within the house they heard vehement trampling, and a sudden shriek of dismay and fury from Mrs Flitch. To add to the confusion, the Rectory poltergeist, roused by these untoward happenings from its diurnal lethargy, came suddenly into action; objects began to fly out of the upstairs windows-pebbles, a comb, a box of *Nuits d'extase*, books, soap, a reproduction of the Sistine Madonna, a cushion, the detachable top of a small prie-dieu, a vase of flowers, a jade elephant and a pair of white woolen bed-socks. The powder-box came open in midair and showered its contents on the Rector.

"Stop it!" the Rector screamed in a sudden transport of rage. "Stop it, you bloody poltergeist!" But his unclerical admonition was without effect. The poltergeist not only continued to throw things, but set up a mournful wailing as well; though this, Fen thought, might not implausibly be ascribed to Mrs Flitch *in extremis*.

"*Conjuro te!*" shrieked the Rector. "*Conjuro te, Satanas!*" He danced hysterically about, coated with powder and smelling like a perfumery.

The situation, Fen felt, was getting out of hand. And it was not greatly improved by the arrival of the crowd from the Inn, who had heard the cars stop and had come pelting breathlessly round to see what was afoot. They poured into the Rectory garden, uttering dazed, irrelevant questions and skipping about in an attempt to avoid the poltergeist's uninterrupted stream of missiles. The dynamic level of the wailing rose abruptly from *mezzo-piano* to *fortissimo*.

"*In nomine Patris et Filii* and all the rest of it," bawled the Rector, convulsed, "*conjuro te*, do you hear me, damn you."

This will not do, Fen told himself: it is my job to go inside and help Humbleby. But before he could move, someone in the crowd shouted: "Look!" and all eyes turned to the roof. Wolfe, dishevelled and sweating, was emerging from a skylight. And for whatever reason—whether because it had shot its bolt or because the Rector's exorcism had been successful—the poltergeist in this instant desisted: the howling and the showers of missiles ceased. And on the crowd below, perhaps in sympathy, a hush fell—until, like a shell from a cannon, Humbleby burst from the front door.

"Lost him," he shouted; and then, observing the direction of their gaze, ran to join them.

The Rectory roof was pseudo-Gothic—a strange agglomeration of peaks and towers and gables and florid chimney stacks; to move about it, though in some respects risky, was by no means impracticable. And Fen saw now what Wolfe was intending to do. To the left, as you stood facing the house, the high garden wall was over-hung by the sturdy branch of an ancient oak which grew in the next demesne; and this branch reached almost to the guttering of the Rectory roof. A determined man, it was clear, would have no difficulty in getting from the roof onto the branch, and by that means across the wall. And Humbleby was not slow in perceiving this; after no more than a single glance he organised a party of volunteers and dispatched them to mount guard at the foot of the oak.

"Come down, Wolfe," he shouted. "You can't get away."

But Wolfe made no answer; it was, indeed, as if he had not heard. He continued to pick his way carefully across the leads, and in the afternoon sunlight they could see the rain of perspiration gleaming on his ruddy skin. With a short exclamation of impatience, Humbleby beckoned to the constable, and together they disappeared into the house.

And that was when Nemesis played its third and last card.

Wolfe was moving slowly along the very margin of the roof—along a narrow ledge between the lowest titles and the gutter—when from behind a near-by chimney stack a bizarre and striking figure emerged. It wore black suede shoes, cotton underpants, a Canadian lumber-jacket and a rather small cricket-cap; it appeared to be eating a sandwich; and it stood champing its jaws and contemplating Wolfe's laborious progress with avuncular interest.

"It's him," said a voice at Fen's elbow; and the crowd muttered recognition. Turning, Fen saw that Myra was beside him, the non-doing pig crouched in untarnished fidelity at her feet. "It's the lunatic," she said, breathless with excitement.

Fen agreed that it was.

"And just think, my dear, he must have been camping there on the roof ever since he escaped. No wonder they didn't find him."

Fen concurred. "But the question now," he said, "is what he's going to do about Wolfe."

That was, indeed, the question. Wolfe had at last perceived the lunatic, and was standing stock-still. The lunatic examined him thoughtfully and then nodded with great affability. Wolfe nodded back—and his relief was clearly perceptible to those who stood below. He resumed his progress. He came opposite to where, nonchalantly leaning against the chimney stack, Elphinstone stood. On all the watchers there fell a sudden, inexplicable silence.

Then it happened.

Elphinstone lurched forward; from his mouth issued, with fog-horn stridency, the sound "Boo!" Opinions differ as to whether he intended actually to attack Wolfe, and the matter is not now susceptible of investigation. But the effect of his unexpected pounce on the raw nerves of the fugitive was decisive. Wolfe's left foot slipped onto the gutter; with a crack like a gunshot it gave way beneath his weight; he staggered, swayed, his hands clutched at vacancy. With a feeble, high-pitched cry he fell.

The crowd sighed, with the hollow reverberation of many indrawn breaths. Faintly, a woman screamed, and then again there was silence. Fen strode to where Wolfe lay, bent over him, and then stripped off his own jacket and laid it on the vacant, unseeing face.

"His neck's broken," he announced briefly. "There's nothing that can be done for him."

Humbleby and the constable had appeared through the skylight just in time to witness the accident. Their original mission abolished, they devoted their energies to persuading Elphinstone to descend. He consented to this with such readiness as to make their cajolings superfluous, and the constable and a farm-labourer were deputed to restore him to Dr Boysenberry's care. As they passed through the lingering, bemused crowd Fen heard him say:

"Damn it all, the man was criminal; and we're always being told that it's the duty of every citizen to prevent criminals from escaping from justice; and I warn you that if my Fourteen Points are not adopted, Western Europe will be at war again within a decade."

Still chatting sociably, he was led away.

CHAPTER TWENTY-TWO

"JANE PERSIMMONS HAS been deaf since birth," said Fen. "And once one realised that, it became painfully obvious who had killed Bussy."

He scrutinised his audience with pleasure. The process of explaining his cases is not as a rule at all disagreeable to him, but on this occasion his personal disgust at being a member of the Mother of Parliaments deprived his recital of all zest. Moreover, his listeners struck him as being irritatingly unaware of the disaster he had suffered; their complacency offended him. They seemed to imagine that God was in His heaven, and all was right with the world—and from their point of view, no doubt, such optimism was justified... Fen's expression of disapproval deepened to a scowl.

It was half past nine on the Sunday evening, and they were on the lawn of the Fish Inn. The bar was no longer habitable, but, in view of the continuing splendour of the weather, to drink outside was a pleasure rather than an incovenience. A window of the bar was being used as a serving-hatch, and

Jacqueline was behind it. Sitting or lying on the grass in a circle round Fen were Diana, Lord Sanford, Myra and Mr Judd. On the outskirts of the group lurked two other figures, Mr Beaver and Captain Watkyn, both of them oppressed, it seemed, by some testing intellectual or moral quandary. Beyond them, a few villagers stood drinking and arguing about the events of the afternoon.

"The case was a simple one," Fen resumed, "and needn't take long to explain. I can't regard it as one of my successes, because I was so unconscionably slow in seeing the truth. However…

"My first clue came from Bussy's account of the murder of Mrs Lambert; it lay in that special oddity of the affair, which both Bussy and I observed. Suppose I am blackmailing you, Judd; and suppose I become aware that you have recognised me as an individual having special knowledge of your seamy past; and suppose that in view of this I decide you must be killed before you can betray me to the police. What is the one thing, in those circumstances, that I am not likely to do? The answer is obvious: I am not likely to devise a method of murder—such as sending poisoned chocolates through the post—which will leave you a comfortable twelve hours before-hand in which to give me away. If I am to kill you at all, the job must obviously be done as quickly as possible—or the reason for doing it will cease to exist.

"But the blackmailer of Mrs Lambert chose the poisoned chocolates method. And from that it was possible provision-ally to infer that he was not afraid of being betrayed to the police before his device could take effect. And why not? Mrs Lambert's husband was away from home, but the day before she had gone to the police alone—in order to inform them of the blackmail—and there was nothing to stop her doing so again. The only thing I could think of that would stop her was the fact that the blackmailer, the revenant from her past, was actually a member of the local police, and in all probability the head of the organization. Mrs Lambert would then have no one in whom she could confide except her husband—who was away; blackmail, on account of a prostitute's career, is not, after all, the sort of thing one communicates even to one's closest friends. And although you may say that she could have gone with her story to the police in some other district, you have only to picture yourself telling one police superintendent that another is guilty of blackmail to realise that it isn't the sort of task one undertakes lightly. Mrs Lambert, then, decided to wait for the return of her husband before taking any action; and on just such a decision Wolfe, posting the poisoned chocolates, could perfectly rely. So she died, and her information died with her.

"I don't say, of course, that the reasoning I've outlined was by any means conclusive. But it was confirmed by the fact, that, as he told me, Bussy had collected or was about to collect substantial evidence tending to the same verdict. And that was why he, too, had to die. What his evidence was, and what he intended by his overt departure and surreptitious return, we shall never know; but Wolfe clearly regarded it as quite sufficient to make his death a crying necessity.

"You'll remember that when the evidence in connection with Bussy's murder had been sifted, and it had been established that all the rigmarole which pointed to Elphinstone was faked, we were left with one crucial problem: How had the murderer known that Bussy was going to turn up at the golf-course hut at all? How had he known to set his stage, and lay his ambush, in such an unlikely place? The *rendez-vous* had not been conceived until my chance meeting with Bussy, and I myself had suggested it quite out of the blue; so the murderer could not have been aware of it *prior* to that moment. And afterwards—well, I said nothing about it, it was wholly unreasonable to suppose that Bussy did, and there was no possibility of our having been overheard. What, then, had happened?

"It took the attempt on Jane Persimmons' life to enlighten me; and it took the incident of the lost field-glasses, and their secret return, wiped clean of fingerprints, to complete that enlightenment. At long last I realised that Jane Persimmons was deaf. *That* was why she had walked straight into a particularly noisy lorry; *that* was why, lip-reading, she watched one attentively whenever one spoke; *that* was why her accent seemed to us slightly foreign—for consonants of the same group *look* the same when one's pronouncing them, and if you have to learn to speak entirely by lip-reading you're liable to blur and confuse them.

"From that point onwards everything was clear. If you can lip-read, and if you have a pair of field-glasses, you can 'over-hear' conversations going on many hundreds of yards beyond earshot. The Inn's guest-rooms look out on the slope where Bussy and I arranged our *rendez-vous*. And Jane was probably in one of them, and standing by the window, at the relevant time.

"Now, *she* didn't kill Bussy, since she was unconscious at the time. She must therefore have communicated my conversation with Bussy to some other person or persons. And she had precious little time in which to do this, since less than ten minutes later she was knocked down by the lorry, remaining unconscious for nearly four days thereafter. All of that narrowed the field decisively. The only persons Jane Persimmons went near during the brief space of time between the fatal conversation and her accident were Myra, Jacqueline and Wolfe; and there was no time for her to have committed anything to paper. Myra and Jacqueline I could easily exonerate, on four separate counts. They were: (i) the blackmailer of Mrs Lambert was almost certainly a man, an old client of hers; (ii) both Myra and Jacqueline had an unshakeable alibi for the time of Bussy's murder; (iii) ordinary common sense made it inconceivable that they were guilty accomplices of the murderer; and (iv) if they were innocent, and

Jane had informed them of my conversation with Bussy, then they had no possible reason for keeping quiet about it subsequently. It was not in them, then, that Jane Persimmons had confided. And since unquestionably she confided in *somebody*, that somebody can only have been Wolfe."

Fen paused, and Mr Judd said:

"All that is amply clear, I think. And it is corroborated beyond all possible doubt by the attempt to kill Jane Persimmons. That, I take it, became necessary as soon as it was obvious that the scheme of implicating Elphinstone had failed.

"Quite so," said Fen. "At first it seemed that Jane might die of her own accord, but as soon as it became likely that she would recover, Wolfe was impelled to silence her; for if she recovered, she would be in a position to publish the utterly damning fact that he knew of my *rendez-vous* with Bussy."

"And the field-glasses," said Mr Judd. "I presume that she picked them up when she was out that day and brought them back here with her, intending to return them to the Rector."

"Exactly. And Wolfe removed them from her room when he visited it on the evening of the accident."

Myra said: "Then was it him, my dear, who wiped them and put them back in the Rector's study?"

"Yes. He wouldn't want to give us any chance of suspecting that Jane was deaf, and therefore in a position to know of the golf-course *rendez-vous* and to hand on the information to him."

"There's only one thing I don't understand," said Mr Judd. "I can visualise Jane, out of idle curiosity, 'overhearing' your conversation with Bussy. But I can't see why she should tell Wolfe about it."

Fen smiled. "You must remember that to her I was at that time an unknown quantity, while Bussy was patently not what he pretended to be. She couldn't know that in our grotesque fashion we represented the Law; on the contrary, we must have seemed to her decidedly suspicious characters. And up to the moment when, the Church clock striking six, Myra interrupted her, this is what she heard—or rather, saw:

'I hadn't hoped to find you so easily. Fen, I need help. You must help me. There's a small element of risk, I'm afraid, but you won't mind that.'

'No, I shan't mind that.'

'Good. It's to do with this Lambert affair, of course. Something I can't manage single-handed. I can't give you the details now, I'm afraid, because I've got to catch a train.'

'You're leaving?'

'To all appearances, yes. I want it to be thought that I've returned to London. But after dark I shall sneak back again, and you must meet me. I can explain the position then.'

'And where do you propose spending the night?'

'In the open.'

'That will be cold and disagreeable. You ought to find a shelter of some kind—if you're proposing to sleep, that is.'

'All right. No doubt a haystack or a barn—'

'Or you might try one of the huts on the golf course.'

'Whatever you say. That would certainly have the advantage of providing a locus in quo for our meeting.'

'And the time?'

'Let's say midnight. I shall almost certainly be back by then, but if I'm not, wait for me.'

'Yes. I suggest the hut at the fourth green. It's reasonably commodious.'

'That will do.'

"Well, at best it was an equivocal sounding interchange; we might have been planning to commit a burglary; and it's not therefore surprising that when, on emerging from the Inn, Jane saw a police officer tinkering with his car, she should feel it her duty to tell him about it.

"The case against Wolfe, then, was conclusive; no other explanation would cover all the facts. And thereafter it was easy to visualise how events looked from his angle. He came to this district about two months ago; he recognised Mrs Lambert; he wanted money (who doesn't?); he decided to blackmail the woman, thinking that after so brief and professional contact with her so many years before she would never remember him. His first demand was met; he sent a second. And then the whole scheme collapsed when she visited the police station to inform the Law of what was going on.

"Undoubtedly he himself interviewed her on that occasion; she recognised him—and must have hurriedly fabricated a false pretext for her presence there. But such recognition is not easily disguised, and such fabrications ring hollow. He knew that she knew him; he knew why she had come to the police; he knew he must silence her in order to escape gaol. Secure in the knowledge that she would take no action till her husband returned, he sent the poisoned chocolates. She died—and he, 'investigating' the case, had ample opportunity to destroy any evidence against him which might remain.

"He must have thought himself completely safe; the shock of learning that Bussy was on his tail must have been severe. How he learned it we don't know, but learn it he undeniably did. Murder breeds murder; Bussy constituted a second and graver threat to his security, so Bussy, too, had to die. When Jane Persimmons told him of my conversation with Bussy, of the golf course meeting-place, he saw his opportunity. The knife was stolen that evening from Judd's house, with trimmings to suggest that Elphinstone had stolen it (the details of Elphinstone's lunacy, remember, were given to the police at the time of his escape). At the golf-course hut, the scene was set. As regards the pince-nez, I imagine that Elphinstone dropped them somewhere and that Wolfe subsequently picked them up, but the point isn't important. It was a clever idea, this attempt to shift the responsibility onto the lunatic; and but for the unavoidable mistake of the fire it would, the way things were going, have almost certainly succeeded. So Bussy died, and Wolfe escaped to his home in time to be called out to 'investigate' the second of his murders.

"But my discovery of Boysenberry's reticence about Elphinstone's phobia reopened the case. It was now Jane who was the danger. For a day or two it seemed that she was going to die as a result of the accident, but on Wednesday the news was abroad that she was better. That night he made his attempt on her life—an attempt so framed as to make it appear that death had been natural. It failed, and he found himself in the ironic position of having to organise precautions against himself. No doubt he intended ultimately to evade those precautions and finish the job. But by yesterday morning the main outlines of the affair were clear to me. I needed time in which to tidy up the loose ends, so I went to Wolfe and spun him a long and circumstantial tale about Myra having killed Bussy—sorry, Myra—with the idea of lulling him into a false sense of security. Whether it did or not I haven't the slightest idea, but in any event I got my breathing-space. When he was confronted by the warrant, his nerve failed him, and then—" Fen shrugged—"well, the rest you know."

(HAPTER TWENTY-THREE

THERE WAS A prolonged silence when he had finished speaking. It was growing dark. The crescent light of a moon just past the full was chasing the last red streaks of the sunset down over the western horizon. The birds, their nightly valedictions completed, were silent. A silver mantle began to take shape on the tree-tops. All colour drained away, leaving only the black and white of a harlequinade. In a near-by coppice Philomela, deliquescent in grief, mourned the infidelity of Tereus and the unshareable joys of Procne.

A little stiffly, Myra got to her feet. "Time, gentlemen, please," she called, "Time, gentlemen, *please.*"

With deliberation the villagers finished their drinks and departed, their voices receding along the road.

"I'm tellin' 'ee, Fred, that ketch, 'er's luffin'."

"Danged if oi think Bert knows what luffin' is."

"Ah. Tell us what 'tis, Bert."

"Why, luffin', 'tis when a yacht goes zigzag to catch the wind."

"Tackin', 'e means."

"When oi mean bloody tackin', oi'll say bloody tackin'."

"Now, see 'ere, that brig..."

The voices were annihilated in the distance. On the lawn of the Inn the group surrounding Fen alone remained, lulled by the nascent magic of the summer night into oblivion of such squalid enactments as the Licensing Laws. Groaning slightly with the effort, Mr Judd rose and crossed to the window of the bar to talk to Jacqueline; his interest in politics, Fen thought, seemed to have evaporated as quickly as it had begun; he had reverted, by a Circean metamorphosis, to the mild and diffident little man whose unpromising exterior enshrined the lurid imagination of Annette de la Tour.

Clearing his throat uneasily, Captain Watkyn said:

"It's just as well the affair ended as it did. Saved a lot of trouble and expense. And you never know what'll happen when these things come into courts. A court of law's not much better than a den of iniquity, in my opinion."

"Or a din of inequity, of course," said Fen. "Myra, have you any champagne?"

"There's half a dozen bottles of Heidsieck in the cellar, my dear."

"Then let's empty them. I need cheering up."

"Well, it's appropriate really, isn't it?" said Myra. "What with Diana and Lord Sanford getting engaged, and now Mr Judd and Jacqueline."

"Mr Judd and Jacqueline?" Fen was startled.

"Oh, yes, my dear. Didn't you know? He asked her this afternoon, and she accepted."

"What a waste of Jacqueline," said Fen, disgusted.

"Well, my dear, most marriages are a waste one way or another, aren't they?"

"I suppose so," said Fen rather drearily. "What has happened about Samuel, Myra? Did you succumb to that evil-smelling chicken?"

"I did not." Myra was firm. "And poor old Samuel's met his Waterloo since then."

"His Waterloo?"

"His wife," Myra explained, "has broken his jaw for him."

"Good God!" This brutal intelligence momentarily roused Fen. "I suppose he deserved it, but still...She didn't try to attack you, did she?"

"Oh, no, my dear. She wasn't annoyed with me. She came round and talked to me about it, friendly like. 'I don't mind 'im rolling in the bushes with the village girls,' she said, 'but I'm not going to have him pestering respectable women like you, Mrs Herbert.'"

"Very proper," Fen murmured. "Very proper indeed."

"Well, I'll get the champagne, then," said Myra, and departed.

Fen relapsed into brooding. It appeared to his peevish imagination that everyone had come well out of the week's events except himself. Humbleby, by now on his way back to London, could feel nothing but satisfaction at so conclusive a finish to the case. Diana and Lord Sanford were united at last. Jane Persimmons—whom they had seen that afternoon—was much better, and would almost certainly be persuaded to settle down with them. Mr Judd was to have the freedom of Jacqueline (Fen found himself unable to conceive the affair in terms more elevated than these) and Jacqueline had presumably some arcane justification for being satisfied with this arrangement. Captain Watkyn had achieved a professional triumph in the face of considerable odds. Boysenberry's reputation was more or less salvaged. Elphinstone would again be receiving such treatment as his egregious condition required. Mr Beaver had largely succeeded in his object of destroying his own Inn.

Olive and Harry Hitchin would be mollocking in some secluded spot, their enjoyment impaired only by the remote possibility of Olive's father coming at them with a knife. Myra was neither better nor worse off than she had been before. The Rector's poltergeist was now public property, and the Psychical Research Society would be after him at any moment, but that was no more than he deserved for deceiving Mrs Flitch. Constable Sly had been lightly wounded, but that was on account of his own stupidity, and in any case he would be about again in a day or two...Fen gazed at the stars, and enquired of them wordlessly why he alone should be afflicted with such condign and unmerited punishment.

Captain Watkyn loomed up at him.

"Look here, old boy, there's something I've got to tell you," said Captain Watkyn.

"If it's about the election," said Fen, "I don't want to hear it."

"Well, yes, it is, but you've just got to hear it, d'you see... You know the law only allows you to spend a certain amount of money on election expenses?"

"Yes, I'm aware of that, thank you."

"Well, I forgot to carry nineteen pounds."

"Watkyn, what are you talking about?"

"I forgot," Captain Watkyn repeated stoically, "to carry nineteen pounds. From the units to the tens. So we've spent seven pounds more than we ought to have done, and the Returning Officer's pounced on it. I'm sorry, old boy, but I'm afraid you're disqualified. And the other two tied, so the Returning Officer has the casting vote, and he's a Conservative, and that's why he's being so nasty about what after all is only a ruddy silly little technical error...You might," Captain Watkyn suggested gloomily, "go to law about it."

Fen shook him warmly by the hand. "Have a drink, Watkyn," he said.

"You mean you don't mind?" said Captain Watkyn dazedly.

"Your mathematical incompetence has probably saved my reason."

"I don't understand it," said Captain Watkyn with pathos. "I just don't understand a single thing about the whole extraordinary business."

The champagne was brought. The glasses were filled. "A toast," said Fen, "to those who are to be married." They drank.

"And now"—Fen's eye lit upon the despondent and taciturn figure of Mr Beaver—"a toast to the rejuvenation of the Fish Inn."

In the moonlight Mr Beaver wanly smiled.

They raised their glasses.

"To the rejuvenation of the Fish Inn," they said.

The ground trembled under them. In the back wall of the Inn a crack appeared, widened, gaped. There was a sound of smashing glass. The chimney pots toppled and the tiles fell like rain. With an earthquake roar, in an enveloping mushroom of dust, the walls of the Fish Inn bulged and collapsed.

Upon the wreck of his hopes Mr Beaver stood staring with incredulous horror.

"This damned government," he whispered. "Oh, this damned *government*."

The villagers assembled to view the prodigy; but in an hour or two, tiring of the spectacle, they returned to their beds. Like looters in a devastated city, Fen's party wandered among the ruins in the moonlight, their champagne glasses still in their hands. Then Diana and Lord Sanford melted away into the night, and Mr Judd and Jacqueline followed them, and the simultaneous disappearance of Myra and Captain Watkyn suggested that they, too, had resolved to make much of time. Fen was left alone with Mr Beaver, who sat on the iron roller at the edge of the lawn with his head hurried in his hands, and who in this emergency would not,

Fen thought, be very congenial company...He went to see if his car was undamaged. It was. A jagged lump of stone, he observed, had given the non-doing pig its quietus, but he did not feel impelled to mourn; the non-doing pig's fidelity had in his opinion never adequately compensated for its basic lack of charm. Fen climbed into the car and drove to Sanford Morvel to look for a room for the night.